Adam Craig

The Casket of Poetical Gems

Choice Standard Selections - Lines and Couplets - Album Verses

Adam Craig

The Casket of Poetical Gems
Choice Standard Selections - Lines and Couplets - Album Verses

ISBN/EAN: 9783337277352

Printed in Europe, USA, Canada, Australia, Japan

Cover: Foto ©Andreas Hilbeck / pixelio.de

More available books at **www.hansebooks.com**

" Listen to the water-mill
Through the live-long day."

(See Page 122.)

THE CASKET

OF

POETICAL GEMS

Choice Standard Selections.

Lines and Couplets.

Album Verses.

COMPILED BY A. CRAIG.

Chicago: W. G. Holmes, 77 Madison St.

1880.

OREN BROS. & CO. ELECTROTYPERS. CHICAGO.

CONTENTS.

CONTENTS.

INDEX OF FIRST LINES.

FULL PAGE ILLUSTRATIONS.

→✠THE✠MAY✠QUEEN.✠←

BY ALFRED TENNYSON.

YOU must wake and call me early, call me
    early, mothei dear;
To-morrow 'ill be the happiest time of all
    the glad New-year;
Of all the glad New-year mother, the
    maddest merriest day;
For I'm to be Queen o' the May, mother,
    I'm to be Queen o' the May.

There's many a black black eye, they say,
    but none so bright as mine;
There's Margaret and Mary, there's Kate
    and Caroline:
But none so fair as little Alice in all the land they say,
So I'm to be Queen o' the May, mother, I'm to be Queen
    o' the May.

I sleep so sound all night, mother, that I shall never wake,
If you do not call me loud when the day begins to break:
But I must gather knots of flowers, and buds and garlands
    gay,
For I'm to be Queen o' the May, mother, I'm to be Queen
    o' the May.

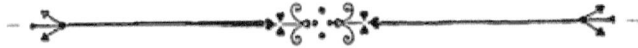

As I came up the valley whom think ye should I see,
But Robin leaning on the bridge beneath the hazel-tree?
He thought of that sharp look, mother, I gave him yesterday—
But I'm to be Queen o' the May, mother, I'm to be Queen
      o' the May.

He thought I was a ghost, mother, for I was all in white,
And I ran by him without speaking, like a flash of light.
They call me cruel-hearted, but I care not what they say,
For I'm to be Queen o' the May, mother, I'm to be Queen
      o' the May.

They say he's dying all for love, but that can never be:
They say his heart is breaking, mother—what is that to me?
There's many a bolder lad 'ill woo me any summer day,
And I'm to be Qeeen o' the May, mother, I'm to be Queen
      o' the May.

Little Effie shall go with me to-morrow to the green,
And you'll be there, too, mother, to see me made the Queen;
For the shepherd lads on every side 'ill come from far away,
And I'm to be Queen o' the May, mother, I'm to be Queen
      o' the May.

The honeysuckle round the porch has wov'n its wavy bowers,
And by the meadow-trenches blow the faint sweet cuckoo-
      flowers;
And the wild marsh-marigold shines like fire in swamps and
      hollows gray,
And I'm to be Queen o' the May, mother, I'm to be Queen
      o' the May.

" And the rivulet in the flowery dale 'ill
Merrily glance and play."

The night-winds come and go, mother, upon the meadow-
    grass,
And the happy stars above them seem to brighten as they
    pass;
There will not be a drop of rain the whole of the livelong
    day,
And I'm to be Queen o' the May, mother, I'm to be Queen
    o' the May.

All the valley, mother, 'ill be fresh and green and still,
And the cowslip and the crowfoot are over all the hill,
And the rivulet in the flowery dale 'ill merrily glance and
    play,
For I'm to be Queen o' the May, mother, I'm to be Queen
    o' the May.

So you must wake and call me early, call me early, mother
    dear,
To-morrow 'ill be the happiest time of all the glad New-year:
To-morrow 'ill be of all the year the maddest merriest day,
For I'm to be Queen o' the May, mother, I'm to be Queen
    o' the May.

NEW-YEAR'S EVE.

IF you're waking, call me early, call me early, mother dear,
For I would see the sun rise upon the glad New-year.
It is the last New-year that I shall ever see,
Then you may lay me low i' the mould and think no more
     of me.

To-night I saw the sun set: he set and left behind
The good old year, the dear old time, and all my peace of
     mind;
And the New-year's coming up, mother, but I shall never see
The blossom on the blackthorn, the leaf upon the tree.

Last May we made a crown of flowers: we had a merry day;
Beneath the hawthorn on the green they made me Queen of
     May;
And we danced about the may-pole and in the hazel copse,
Till Charles's Wain came out above the tall white chimney-
     tops.

There's not a flower on all the hills; the frost is on the pane:
I only wish to live till the snowdrops come again:
I wish the snow would melt and the sun come out on high:
I long to see a flower so before the day I die.

The building rook 'ill caw from the windy tall elm-tree,
And the tufted plover pipe along the fallow lea,

And the swallow 'ill come back again with summer o'er the
        wave,
But I shall lie alone, mother, within the mouldering grave.

Upon the chancel-casement, and upon that grave of mine,
In the early early morning the summer sun 'ill shine,
Before the red cock crows from the farm upon the hill,
When you are warm-asleep, mother, and all the world is still.

When the flowers come again, mother, beneath the waning
    light
You'll never see me more in the long gray fields at night:
When from the dry dark wold the summer airs blow cool
On the oat-grass and the sword-grass, and the bulrush in the
    pool.

You'll bury me, my mother, just beneath the hawthorn shade,
And you'll come sometimes and see me where I am lowly laid.
I shall not forget you, mother, I shall hear you when you pass,
With your feet above my head in the long and pleasant grass.

I have been wild and wayward, but you'll forgive me now;
You'll kiss me, my own mother, and forgive me ere I go;
Nay, nay, you must not weep, nor let your grief be wild,
You should not fret for me, mother, you have another child.

If I can I'll come again, mother, from out my resting-place;
Tho' you'll not see me, mother, I shall look upon your face;
Tho' I cannot speak a word, I shall hearken what you say,
And be often, often with you when you think I'm far away.

Good-night, good-night, when I have said good-night for-
    evermore,
And you see me carried out from the threshold of the door;
Don't let Effie come to see me till my grave be growing green;
She'll be a better child to you than I have ever been.

She'll find my garden-tools upon the granary floor;
Let her take 'em: they are hers: I shall never garden more:
But tell her, when I'm gone, to train the rose-bush that I set
About the parlor-window and the box of mignonette.

Good-night, sweet mother; call me before the day is born,
All night I lie awake, but I fall asleep at morn;
But I would see the sun rise upon the glad New-year,
So, if you're waking, call me, call me early, mother dear.

CONCLUSION.

I THOUGHT to pass away before, and yet alive I am;
And in the fields all round I hear the bleating of the lamb.
How sadly, I remember, rose the morning of the year!
To die before the snowdrop came, and now the violet's here.

O sweet is the new violet, that comes beneath the skies,
And sweeter is the young lamb's voice to me that cannot rise,
And sweet is all the land about, and all the flowers that blow,
And sweeter far is death than life to me that long to go.

It seem'd so hard at first, mother, to leave the blessed sun,
And now it seems as hard to stay, and yet His will be done!
But still I think it can't be long before I find release;
And that good man, the clergyman, has told me words of
        peace.

O blessings on his kindly voice and on his silver hair!
And blessings on his whole life long, until he meet me there!
O blessings on his kindly heart and on his silver head!
A thousand times I blest him, as he knelt beside my bed.

He taught me all the mercy, for he show'd me all the sin.
Now, tho' my lamp was lighted late, there's One will let me in;
Nor would I now be well, mother, again, if that could be,
For my desire is but to pass to Him that died for me.

I did not hear the dog howl, mother, or the death-watch beat,
There came a sweeter token when the night and morning meet;
But sit beside my bed, mother, and put your hand in mine,
And Effie on the other side, and I will tell the sign.

All in the wild March-morning I heard the angels call:
It was when the moon was setting, and the dark was over all;
The trees began to whisper, and the wind began to roll,
And in the wild March-morning I heard them call my soul.

For lying broad awake I thought of you and Effie dear;
I saw you sitting in the house, and I no longer here;
With all my strength I pray'd for both, and so I felt resigned,
And up the valley came a swell of music on the wind.

I thought that it was fancy, and I listen'd in my bed,
And then did something speak to me—I know not what was
    said;
For great delight and shuddering took hold of all my mind,
And up the valley came again the music on the wind.

But you were sleeping: and I said, " It's not for them: it's
    mine."
And if it comes three times, I thought, I take it for a sign.
And once again it came, and close beside the window-bars,
Then seem'd to go right up to Heaven and die among the
    stars.

So now I think my time is near. I trust it is. I know
The blessed music went that way my soul will have to go.
And for myself, indeed, I care not if I go to-day.
But Effie, you must comfort *her* when I am past away.

And say to Robin a kind word, and tell him not to fret;
There's many worthier than I, would make him happy yet.
If I had lived—I cannot tell—I might have been his wife;
But all these things have ceased to be, with my desire of life.

O look ! the sun begins to rise, the heavens are in a glow;
He shines upon a hundred fields, and all of them I know.
And there I move no longer now, and there his light may
    shine—
Wild flowers in the valley for other hands than mine.

O sweet and strange it seems to me, that ere this day is done
The voice, that now is speaking, may be beyond the sun—
For ever and for ever with those just souls and true—
And what is life, that we should moan ? why make we such
    ado ?

For ever and for ever, all in a blessed home—
And there to wait a little while till you and Effie come—
To lie within the light of God, as I lie upon your breast—
And the wicked cease from troubling, and the weary are at
    rest.

→⁙ELEGY⁙←

WRITTEN ÷ IN ÷ A ÷ COUNTRY ÷ CHURCHYARD.

By Thomas Gray.

THE Curfew tolls the knell of parting day;
　　The lowing herd winds slowly o'er the lea;
　The ploughman homeward plods his weary way,
　　And leaves the world to darkness and to me.

　　Now fades the glimmering landscape on the sight,
　　　And all the air a solemn stillness holds,
Save where the beetle wheels his droning flight,
　　And drowsy tinklings lull the distant folds:

Save that, from yonder ivy-mantled tower,
　　The moping Owl does to the Moon complain
Of such as, wandering near her secret bower,
　　Molest her ancient solitary reign.

Beneath those rugged elms, that yew-tree's shade,
　　Where heaves the turf in many a mouldering heap,
Each in his narrow cell for ever laid,
　　The rude forefathers of the hamlet sleep.

The breezy call of incense-breathing Morn,
    The swallow twittering from the straw-built shed,
The cock's shrill clarion, or the echoing horn,
    No more shall rouse them from their lowly bed.

For them, no-more the blazing hearth shall burn,
    Or busy housewife ply her evening care;
No children run to lisp their sire's return,
    Or climb his knees, the envied kiss to share.

Oft did the harvest to their sickle yield;
    Their furrow oft the stubborn glebe has broke;
How jocund did they drive their team a-field !
    How bow'd the woods beneath their sturdy stroke !

Let not Ambition mock their useful toil,
　　Their homely joys, and destiny obscure;
Nor Grandeur hear, with a disdainful smile,
　　The short and simple annals of the poor.

The boast of heraldry, the pomp of power,
　　And all that beauty, all that wealth, e'er gave,
Await, alike, th' inevitable hour;—
　　The paths of glory lead but to the grave.

Nor you, ye proud ! impute to these the fault,
　　If memory o'er their tomb no trophies raise;
Where, through the long-drawn aisle and fretted vault,
　　The pealing anthem swells the note of praise.

Can storied urn, or animated bust,
　　Back to its mansion call the fleeting breath ?
Can Honor's voice provoke the silent dust ?
　　Or Flattery soothe the dull cold ear of Death ?

Perhaps, in this neglected spot, is laid
　　Some heart, once pregnant with celestial fire;
Hands, that the rod of empire might have sway'd,
　　Or wak'd to ecstasy the living lyre.

But Knowledge, to their eyes, her ample page,
　　Rich with the spoils of Time, did ne'er unroll;
Chill Penury repress'd their noble rage,
　　And froze the genial current of the soul.

Full many a gem of purest ray serene
　　The dark unfathom'd caves of ocean bear;
Full many a flower is born to blush unseen,
　　And waste its sweetness on the desert air.

Some village Hampden, that, with dauntless breast,
     The little tyrant of his fields withstood;
Some mute, inglorious Milton,—here may rest;
     Some Cromwell, guiltless of his country's blood.

Th' applause of listening senates to command;
     The threats of pain and ruin to despise;
To scatter plenty o'er a smiling land,
     And read their history in a nation's eyes,

Their lot forbad: nor circumscrib'd alone
     Their growing virtues, but their crimes confin'd;
Forbad to wade through slaughter to a throne,
     And shut the gates of mercy on mankind.

The struggling pangs of conscious truth to hide;
     To quench the blushes of ingenuous shame;
Or heap the shrine of Luxury and Pride,
     With incense kindled at the Muse's flame.

Far from the madding crowd's ignoble strife,
     Their sober wishes never learn'd to stray;
Along the cool, sequester'd vale of life,
     They kept the noiseless tenor of their way.

Yet e'en these bones from insult to protect,
     Some frail memorial still erected high,
With uncouth rhymes and shapeless sculpture deck'd,
     Implores the passing tribute of a sigh.

Their name, their years, spelt by th' unletter'd Muse,
     The place of fame and elegy supply;
And many a holy text around she strews,
     That teach the rustic moralist to die.

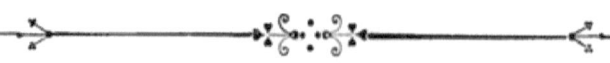

For who, to dumb Forgetfulness a prey,
    This pleasing, anxious being e'er resign'd;
Left the warm precincts of the cheerful day,
    Nor cast one longing, lingering look behind?

On some fond breast the parting soul relies;
    Some pious drops the closing eye requires;
E'en from the tomb the voice of Nature cries;
    E'en in our ashes live their wonted fires.

For thee, who, mindful of th' unhonor'd dead,
    Dost in these lines their artless tale relate;
If, 'chance, by lonely Contemplation led,
    Some kindred spirit shall inquire thy fate;

Haply, some hoary-headed swain may say:
    " Oft have we seen him, at the peep of dawn,
Brushing, with hasty steps, the dews away,
    To meet the Sun upon the upland lawn.

" There, at the foot of yonder nodding beech,
    That wreathes its old fantastic roots so high,
His listless length, at noontide, would he stretch,
    And pore upon the brook that babbles by.

Hard by yon wood, now smiling, as in scorn,
    Muttering his wayward fancies, he would rove;
Now drooping, woeful, wan, like one forlorn,
    Or craz'd with care, or cross'd in hopeless love.

" One morn, I miss'd him on the 'customed hill,
    Along the heath, and near his favorite tree;
Another came,—nor yet beside the rill,
    Nor up the lawn, nor at the wood, was he;

" 'The next, with dirges due, in sad array,
    Slow through the church-way path we saw him borne,
Approach and read (for thou canst read) the lay
    Grav'd on the stone beneath yon aged thorn."

Here rests his head upon the lap of Earth,
    A youth, to fortune and to fame unknown;
Fair Science frown'd not on his humble birth,
    And melancholy mark'd him for her own.

Large was his bounty, and his soul sincere;   .
    Heaven did a recompense as largely send:
He gave to Misery all he had—a tear;
    He gain'd from Heaven ('twas all he wish'd) a friend.

No further seek his merits to disclose,
    Or draw his frailties from their dread abode:
(There they alike in trembling hope repose,)
    The bosom of his Father and his God.

➤❖LOVE.❖◄

By Samuel Taylor Coleridge.

ALL thoughts, all passions, all delights,
Whatever stirs this mortal frame,
Are all but ministers of Love,
    And feed his sacred flame.

Oft in my waking dreams do I
Live o'er again, that happy hour,
When midway on the mount I lay,
    Beside the ruined tower.

The moonshine, stealing o'er the scene
Had blended with the light of eve;
And she was there, my hope, my joy,
    My own dear Genevieve!

She leaned against the armed man,
The statue of the armed knight;
She stood and listened to my lay,
    Amid the lingering light.

Few sorrows hath she of her own,
My hope! my joy! my Genevieve!
She loves me best, whene'er I sing
      The songs that make her grieve.

I played a soft and doleful air,
I sang an old and moving story—
An old rude song, that suited well
      That ruin wild and hoary.

She listened with a flitting blush,
With downcast eyes and modest grace;
For well she knew, I could not choose
      But gaze upon her face.

I told her of the Knight that wore
Upon his shield a burning brand;
And that for ten long years he wooed
      The Lady of the Land.

I told her how he pined: and ah!
The deep, the low, the pleading tone
With which I sang another's love,
      Interpreted my own.

She listened with a flitting blush,
With downcast eyes, and modest grace;
And she forgave me, that I gazed
      Too fondly on her face!

GENEVIEVE.

But when I told the cruel scorn
That crazed that bold and lovely Knight,
And that he crossed the mountain-woods,
　　Nor rested day nor night;

That sometimes from the savage den,
And sometimes from the darksome shade,
And sometimes starting up at once
　　In green and sunny glade,—

There came and looked him in the face
An angel beautiful and bright;
And that he knew it was a Fiend,
　　This miserable Knight!

And that, unknowing what he did,
He leaped amid a murderous band,
And saved from outrage worse than death
　　The Lady of the Land;—

And how she wept, and clasped his knees;
And how she tended him in vain—
And ever strove to expiate
　　The scorn that crazed his brain;—

And that she nursed him in a cave;
And how his madness went away,
When on the yellow forest-leaves
　　A dying man he lay;

—His dying words—but when I reached
The tenderest strain of all the ditty,
My faltering voice and pausing harp
　　Disturbed her soul with pity.

All impulses of soul and sense
Had thrilled my guileless Genevieve;
The music and the doleful tale,
    The rich and balmy eve;

And hopes, and fears that kindle hope,
An undistinguishable throng,
And gentle wishes long subdued,
    Subdued, and cherished long !

She wept with pity and delight,
She blushed with love, and virgin shame;
And like the murmur of a dream,
    I heard her breathe my name.

Her bosom heaved—she stepped aside,
As conscious of my look she stept—
Then suddenly, with timorous eye,
    She fled to me and wept.

She half inclosed me with her arms,
She pressed me with a meek embrace;
And bending back her head, looked up,
    And gazed upon my face.

'Twas partly love, and partly fear,
And partly 'twas a bashful art,
That I might rather feel, than see,
    The swelling of her heart.

I calmed her fears, and she was calm,
And told her love with virgin pride;
And so I won my Genevieve,
    My bright and beauteous Bride.

OH, WHY SHOULD THE SPIRIT OF MORTAL ⇸✳BE PROUD?✳⇽

By WILLIAM KNOX.

H, why should the spirit of mortal be proud?
Like a swift fleeting meteor, a fast-flying cloud,
A flash of the lightning, a break of the wave,
Man passeth from life to his rest in the grave.

The leaves of the oak and the willow shall fade,
Be scattered around and together be laid;
And the young and the old, and the low and the high,
Shall moulder to dust and together shall lie.

The infant a mother attended and loved;
The mother that infant's affection who proved;
The husband that mother and infant who blessed,
Each, all, are away to their dwellings of rest.

The maid on whose cheek, on whose brow, in whose eye,
Shone beauty and pleasure,—her triumphs are by;
And the memory of those who loved her and praised,
Are alike from the minds of the living erased.

The hand of the king that the sceptre hath borne;
The brow of the priest that the mitre hath worn;
The eye of the sage and the heart of the brave,
Are hidden and lost in the depth of the grave.

The peasant whose lot was to sow and to reap;
The herdsman, who climbed with his goats up the steep;
The beggar, who wandered in search of his bread,
Have faded away like the grass that we tread.

The saint who enjoyed the communion of heaven,
The sinner who dared to remain unforgiven,
The wise and the foolish, the guilty and just,
Have quietly mingled their bones in the dust.

So the multitude goes, like the flower or the weed
That withers away to let others succeed;
So the multitude comes, even those we behold,
To repeat every tale that has often been told.

For we are the same our fathers have been;
We see the same sights our fathers have seen,—
We drink the same stream and view the same sun,
And run the same course our fathers have run.

The thoughts we are thinking our fathers would think;
From the death we are shrinking our fathers would shrink;
To the life we are clinging they also would cling;
But it speeds for us all, like a bird on the wing.

They loved, but the story we cannot unfold;
They scorned, but the heart of the haughty is cold;
They grieved, but no wail from their slumbers will come;
They joyed, but the tongue of their gladness is dumb.

They died, ay! they died: and we things that are now,
Who walk on the turf that lies over their brow,
Who make in their dwelling a transient abode,
Meet the things that they met on their pilgrimage road.

Yea! hope and despondency, pleasure and pain,
We mingle together in sunshine and rain;
And the smiles and the tears, the song and the dirge,
Still follow each other, like surge upon surge.

'Tis the wink of an eye, 'tis the draught of a breath,
From the blossom of health to the paleness of death,
From the gilded saloon to the bier and the shroud,—
Oh, why should the spirit of mortal be proud?

➤✳THE✦LAST✦MAN.✳⬅

By Thomas Campbell.

ALL worldly shapes shall melt in gloom;
 The Sun himself must die,
Before this mortal shall assume
 Its immortality!
I saw a vision in my sleep,
That gave my spirit strength to sweep
 Adown the gulf of Time!
I saw the last of human mould
That shall Creation's death behold,
 As Adam saw her prime.

The Sun's eye had a sickly glare,
 The Earth with age was wan,
The skeletons of nations were
 Around that lonely man!
Some had expired in fight—the brands
Still rusted in their bony hands;
 In plague and famine some!
Earth's cities had no sound nor tread,
And ships were drifting with the dead
 To shores where all was dumb!

" Yet, prophet-like, that lone one stood,
  With dauntless words and high."

Yet, prophet-like, that lone one stood,
  With dauntless words and high,
That shook the sere leaves from the wood,
  As if a storm passed by;
Saying, " We are twins in death, proud Sun,
Thy face is cold, thy race is run—
  'Tis mercy bids thee go;
For thou ten thousand, thousand years
Hast seen the tide of human tears,
  That shall no longer flow.

" What though beneath thee man put forth
  His pomp, his pride, his skill;
And arts that made fire, flood, and earth,
  The vassals of his will !
Yet mourn I not thy parted sway,
Thou dim discrowned* king of day,
  For all these trophied arts
And triumphs, that beneath thee sprang,
Healed not a passion, or a pang,
  Entailed on human hearts.

" Go,—let oblivion's curtain fall
  Upon the stage of men,
Nor with thy rising beams recall
  Life's tragedy again;
Its piteous pageants bring not back,
Nor weaken flesh upon the rack
  Of pain anew to writhe;
Stretched in disease's shapes abhorred,
Or mown in battle by the sword,
  Like grass beneath the scythe.

---

* "My gray, discrowned head."—CHARLES I.

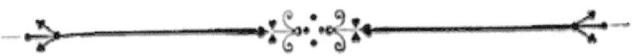

"E'en I am weary in yon skies
    To watch thy fading fire;
Test of all sumless agonies,
    Behold not me expire.
My lips that speak thy dirge of death—
Their rounded gasp and gurgling breath
    To see thou shalt not boast;
The eclipse of Nature spreads my pall—
The majesty of Darkness shall
    Receive my parting ghost !

"This spirit shall return to him
    That gave its heavenly spark;
Yet think not, Sun, it shall be dim
    When thou thyself art dark !
No ! it shall live again, and shine
In bliss unknown to beams of thine,
    By Him recalled to breath,
Who captive led captivity,
Who robbed the Grave of victory,
    And took the sting from Death !

Go, Sun, while Mercy holds me up
    On Nature's awful waste,
To drink this last and bitter cup
    Of grief that man shall taste—
Go, tell the night that hides thy face,
Thou saw'st the last of Adam's race,
    On Earth's sepulchral clod,
The dark'ning universe defy
To quench his immortality,
    Or shake his trust in God ! "

SUMMER.

➤✳SUMMER.✳◄

BY CHRISTINA ROSSETTI.

INTER is cold-hearted;
  Spring is yea and nay;
  Autumn is a weather-cock,
   Blown every way;
  Summer days for me,
  When every leaf is on its tree,

When Robin's not a beggar,
  And Jenny Wren's a bride,
And larks hang, singing, singing, singing,
  Over the wheat-fields wide,
  And anchored lilies ride,
And the pendulum spider
  Swings from side to side,

And blue-black beetles transact business,
  And gnats fly in a host,
And furry caterpillars hasten
  That no time be lost,
And moths grow fat and thrive,
And ladybirds arrive.

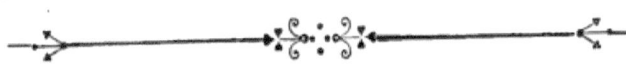

Before green apples blush,
    Before green nuts embrown,
Why, one day in the country
    Is worth a month in town—
    Is worth a day and a year
Of the dusty, musty, lag-last fashion
    That days drone everywhere.

EVELYN HOPE

⟶❊EVELYN❖HOPE.❊⟵

BY ROBERT BROWNING.

I.

EAUTIFUL Evelyn Hope is dead !
 Sit and watch by her side an hour.
That is her book-shelf, this her bed;
 She plucked that geranium-flower,
Beginning to die, too, in the glass;
 Little has yet been changed, I think:
The shutters are shut, no light may pass
 Save two long rays through the hinge and chink.

II.

Sixteen years old when she died !
 Perhaps she had scarcely heard my name;
It was not her time to love; beside,
 Her life had many a hope and aim,
Duties enough and little cares,
 And now was quiet, now astir,
Till God's hand beckoned unawares—
 And the sweet white brow is all of her.

III.

It is too late, then, Evelyn Hope?
    What ! your soul was pure and true,
The good stars met in your horoscope,
    Made you of spirit, fire and dew—
And just because I was thrice as old,
    And our paths in the world diverged so wide,
Each was nought to each, must I be told?
    We were fellow-mortals, nought beside?

IV.

No, indeed ! for God above
    Is great to grant, as mighty to make,
And creates the love to reward the love;
    I claim you still, for my own love's sake !
Delayed it may be for more lives yet,
    Through worlds I shall traverse not a few:
Much is to learn and much to forget
    Ere the time be come for taking you.

V.

But the time will come—at last it will,
    When, Evelyn Hope, what meant (I shall say)
In the lower Earth, in the years long still,
    That body and soul so pure and gay?
Why, your hair was amber, I shall divine,
    And your mouth of your own geranium's red—
And what you would do with me, in fine,
    In the new life come in the old one's stead.

VI.

I have lived (I shall say) so much since then,
    Given up myself so many times,
Gained me the gains of various men,
    Ransacked the ages, spoiled the climes;
Yet one thing, one, in my soul's full scope,
    Either I missed, or itself missed me:
And I want and find you, Evelyn Hope:
    What is the issue? let us see.

VII.

I loved you, Evelyn, all the while!
    My heart seemed full as it could hold—
There was place and to spare for the frank young smile
    And the red young mouth and the hair's young gold,
So, hush—I will give you this leaf to keep—
    See, I shut inside the sweet cold hand.
There, that is our secret: go to sleep;
    You will wake, and remember, and understand.

THE CRY OF THE CHILDREN.

By Elizabeth Barrett Browning.

DO ye hear the children weeping, O my brothers,
    Ere the sorrow comes with years ?
They are leaning their young heads against their
    mothers',
      And *that* cannot stop their tears.
The young lambs are bleating in the meadows,
  The young birds are chirping in the nest,
The young fawns are playing with the shadows,
  The young flowers are blowing towards the west—
But the young, young children, O my brothers,
    They are weeping bitterly !
They are weeping in the playtime of the others,
    In the country of the free.

Do you question the young children in their sorrow
    Why their tears are falling so ?
The old man may weep for his to-morrow,
    Which is lost in Long Ago;
The tree is leafless in the forest,
  The old year is ending with the frost,
The old wound, if stricken, is the sorest,
  The old hope is hardest to be lost:
But the young, young children, O my brothers,
    Do you ask them why they stand
Weeping sore before the bosoms of their mothers,
    In our happy Fatherland ?

They look up with their pale and sunken faces,
　　And their looks are sad to see,
For the man's hoary anguish draws and presses
　　Down the cheeks of infancy;
" Your old Earth," they say, " is very dreary;
　　Our young feet," they say, " are very weak;
Few paces have we taken, yet are weary,—
　　Our grave-rest is very far to seek:
Ask the aged why they weep, and not the children;
　　For the outside Earth is cold,
·And we young ones stand without in our bewildering,
　　And the graves are for the old."

" True," say the children, " it may happen,
　　That we die before our time:
Little Alice died last year; her grave is shapen
　　Like a snowball, in the rime.
We looked into the pit prepared to take her;
　　Was no room for any work in the close clay !
From the sleep wherein she lieth none can wake her,
　　Crying ' Get up, little Alice, it is day ! '
If you listen by that grave in sun and shower,
　　With your ear down, little Alice never cries;
Could we see her face, be sure we should not know her,
　　For the smile has time for growing in her eyes.
And merry go her moments, lulled and stilled in
　　The shroud by the kirk-chime.
It is good when it happens," say the children,
　　" That we die before our time."

Alas, alas, the children ! they are seeking
　　Death in life as best to have:
They are binding up their hearts, away from breaking
　　With a cerement from the grave.

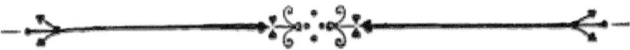

Go out, children, from the mine and from the city,
 Sing out, children, as the little thrushes do;
Pluck your handfuls of the meadow cowslips pretty,
 Laugh loud to feel your fingers let them through !
But they answer, "Are your cowslips of the meadows
  Like our weeds anear the mine ?
Leave us quiet in the dark of the coal-shadows,
  From your pleasures fair and fine !

" For oh," say the children, " we are weary,
 And we cannot run or leap !
If we cared for any meadows, it were merely
 To drop down in them and sleep.
Our knees tremble sorely in the stooping,
 We fall upon our faces trying to go;
And underneath our heavy eyelids drooping
 The reddest flower would look as pale as snow.
For, all day, we drag our burden tiring,
 Through the coal-dark underground;
Or, all day, we drive the wheels of iron
 In the factories, round and round.

" For all day the wheels are droning, turning;
 Their wind comes in our faces,
Till our hearts turn, our head with pulses burning,
 And the walls turn in their places;
Turns the sky in the high window blank and reeling,
 Turns the long light that drops adown the wall,
Turn the black flies that crawl along the ceiling—
 All are turning, all the day, and we with all.
And all the day the iron wheels are droning,
 And sometimes we could pray,
'O ye wheels' (breaking out in a mad moaning),
 'Stop ! be silent for to-day !' "

Ay, be silent! Let them hear each other breathing
    For a moment, mouth to mouth!
Let them touch each other's hands, in a fresh wreathing
    Of their tender human youth!
Let them feel that this cold metallic motion
    Is not all the life God fashions and reveals:
Let them prove their living souls against the notion
    That they live in you, or under you, O wheels!
Still all day the iron wheels go onward,
    Grinding life down from its mark;
And the children's souls, which God is calling sunward,
    Spin on blindly in the dark.

Now tell the poor young children, O my brothers,
    To look up to him and pray;
So the Blessed One, who blesseth all the others,
    Will bless them another day.
They answer, "Who is God that he should hear us,
    While the rushing of the iron wheels is stirred?
When we sob aloud, the human creatures near us
    Pass by, hearing not, or answer not a word;
And we hear not (for the wheels in their resounding)
    Strangers speaking at the door:
Is it likely God, with angels singing round him,
    Hears our weeping any more?

"Two words, indeed, of praying we remember,
    And at midnight's hour of harm,
'Our Father,' looking upward in the chamber,
    We say softly for a charm.
We know no other words except 'Our Father,'
    And we think that, in some pause of angel's song,
God may pluck them with the silence sweet to gather,
    And hold both within his right hand which is strong.

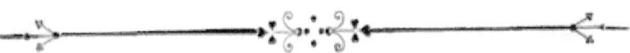

"Our Father !'   If he heard us, he would surely
      (For they call him good and mild)
Answer, smiling down the steep world very purely,
      'Come and rest with me, my child.'

" But no ! " say the children, weeping faster,
      " He is speechless as a stone:
And they tell us, of his image is the master
      'Who commands us to work on.
Go to ! " say the children, " up in heaven
      Dark wheel-like turning clouds are all we find.
Do not mock us, grief has made us unbelieving:
      We look up for God, but tears have made us blind."
Do you hear the children weeping and disproving,
      O my brothers, what ye preach ?
For God's possible is taught by this world's loving,
      And the children doubt of each.

And well may the children weep before you !
      They are weary ere they run;
They have never seen the sunshine, nor the glory
      Which is brighter than the sun.
They know the grief of man, without its wisdom;
      They sink in man's despair, without its calm;
Are slaves, without the liberty in Christdom;
      Are martyrs, by the pang without the palm:
Are worn, as if with age, yet unretrievingly
      The harvest of its memories cannot reap,—
Are orphans of the earthly love and heavenly.
      Let them weep ! let them weep !

They look up with their pale and sunken faces,
      And their look is dread to see;
For they, mind you of their angels in high places,
      With their eyes turned on Deity.

" How long," they say, " how long, O cruel nation,
　　Will you stand, to move the world, on a child's heart,—
Stifle down with a mailed heel its palpitation,
　　And tread onward to your throne amid the mart ?
Our blood splashes upward, O gold-heaper,
　　And your purple shows your path !　•
But the child's sob in the silence curses deeper
　　Than the strong man in his wrath."

→✳LINES✳←

WRITTEN WHILE SAILING IN A BOAT AT EVENING.

BY WORDSWORTH.

OW richly glows the water's breast
    Before us, tinged with evening hues,
While facing thus the crimson west,
    The boat her silent course pursues!
And see how dark the backward stream!
    A little moment past so smiling!
And still, perhaps, with faithless gleam,
    Some other loiterers beguiling.

Such views the youthful bard' allure,
    But heedless of the following gloom,
He deems their colors shall endure
    Till peace go with him to the tomb.
And let him nurse his fond deceit,
    And what if he must die in sorrow!
Who would not cherish dreams so sweet,
    Though grief and pain may come to-morrow!

(46)

" While facing thus the crimson west,
The boat her silent course pursues. "

→✳THE✦NAMELESS✦DEAD.✳←

By Tom·Hood.

HY do you wail, O Wind? why do you sigh,
    O Sea?
Is it remorse for the ships gone down, with this
      pitiless shore on the lea?
    Moan, moan, moan
    In the desolate night and lone!
      Ah, what is the tale
      You would fain unveil
In your wild weird cries to me?

A gleam of white on the shore!—'tis not the white sea-foam,
Nor wandering sea-bird's glimmering wing, for at night no
    sea-birds roam.
        'Tis one of the drowned—drowned
        Of the hapless homeward-bound,
          Last night, in the dark,
          There perish'd a bark
On the bar; and 'twas bound for home!

A woman's cold white corpse—a woman so young and fair!
See, the cruel storm has entwined with weeds the wealth of
    her weltering hair;
        And the little, the little hand
        Lies listless and limp on the sand.
          They have bound her fast
          To the wreck of a mast;
But the wild waves would not spare!

Look, how they bound and leap—cast themselves far o'er
　　the shore,
Striving to seize on their stranded prey, and carry it off once
　　more!
　　　　Or is it remorse or dread,
　　　　Or a longing to bury its dead,
　　　　　　That makes the surge
　　　　　　On the ocean-verge
So incessantly howl and roar?

Where do they list for her step? where do they look for her face?
Where are they waiting to see her once more in the old
　　familiar place?
　　　　Dead, dead, dead!
　　　　In vain will their tears be shed;
　　　　　　For not one of them all,
　　　　　　Alas will fall
On that bosom's marble grace!

Why do you sigh, O Sea? why do you wail, O Wind?
Why do you murmur, in mournful tone, like things with a
　　human mind?
　　　　Wail, wail, wail,
　　　　Articulate ocean and gale!
　　　　　　For the loveliness rare,
　　　　　　So pallid and fair,
You slew in your fury blind!

Let us bear her away to a grave in the churchyard's calm
　　green breast,
Where the sound of the wind and waves in strife may never
　　her peace molest.
　　　　Though we cannot carve her name,
　　　　She will slumber all the same;
　　　　　　And the wild-rose bloom
　　　　　　Shall cover her tomb,
And she shall have perfect rest.

" Why do you wail, O wind?
Why do you sigh, O sea?"

" Where the hedgeside roses blow,
Where the little daisies grow."

TIRED OUT.

E does well who does his best;
Is he weary? let him rest.
Brothers! I have done my best,
I am weary—let me rest.
After toiling oft in vain,
Baffled, yet to struggle fain;
After toiling long, to gain
Little good with mickle pain,
Let me rest.   But lay me low,
Where the hedgeside roses blow;
Where the little daisies grow,
Where the winds a-maying go;
Where the footpath rustics plod;
Where the breeze-bowed poplars nod;
Where the old woods worship God,
Where His pencil paints the sod;
Where the wedded throstle sings,
Where the young bird tries his wings;
Where the wailing plover sings,
Near the runlet's rushing springs!
Where, at times, the tempest's roar,
Shaking distant sea and shore,
Still will rave old Barnesdale o'er,
To be heard by me no more!
There, beneath the breezy west,
Tired and thankful, let me rest,
Like a child that sleepeth best
On its mother's gentle breast.

THE · SENSITIVE · PLANT.

By Percy Bysshe Shelley.

PART I.

A SENSITIVE Plant in a garden grew,
And the young winds fed it with silver dew;
And it opened its fan-like leaves to the light,
And closed them beneath the kisses of night.

And the spring arose on the garden fair,
Like the spirit of love, felt everywhere !
And each flower and herb on earth's dark
    breast
Rose from the dreams of its wintry rest.

The Snowdrop, and then the Violet,
Arose from the ground with warm rain wet;
And their breath was mixed with fresh odor,
    sent
From the turf, like the voice to the instru-
    ment.

Then the pied Wind-flowers, and the Tulip tall,
And Narcissi, the fairest among them all—
Who gaze on their eyes in the stream's recess,
Till they die of their own dear loveliness.

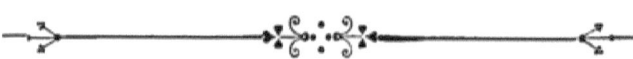

And the naiad-like Lily of the Vale,
Whom youth makes so fair, and passions so pale,
That the light of its tremulous bells is seen
Through their pavilions of tender green.

And the Hyacinth, purple, and white, and blue,
Which flung from its bells a sweet peal anew
Of music so delicate, soft, and intense,
It was felt like an odor within the sense.

And the Rose, like a nymph to the bath addrest,
Which unveiled the depth of her glowing breast,
Till, fold after fold, to the fainting air
The soul of her beauty and love lay bare.

And the wand-like Lily, which lifted up,
As a Mænad, its moonlight-colored cup,
Till the fiery star, which is its eye,
Gazed through clear dew on the tender sky.

And the Jessamine faint, and the sweet Tuberose,
The sweetest flower for scent that blows!
And all rare blossoms, from every clime,
Grew in that garden in perfect prime.

And on the stream, whose inconstant bosom
Was prankt under boughs of embowering blossom,
With golden and green light, and, starting through
Their heaven of many a tangled hue,

Broad Water-lilies lay tremulously,
And starry River-buds glimmered by,
And around them the soft stream did glide and dance
With a motion of sweet sound and radiance.

And the sinuous paths of lawn and moss,
Which led through the garden along and across—
Some open at once to the sun and the breeze,
Some lost among bowers of blossoming trees—

Were all paved with Daisies and delicate bells,
As fair as the fabulous Asphodels,
And flow'rets, drooping as day drooped too,
Fell into pavilions white, purple, and blue,
To roof the glow-worm from the evening dew.

And from this undefiled paradise
The flowers (as an infant's awakening eyes
Smile on its mother, whose singing sweet
Can first lull, and at last must awaken it).

When heaven's blithe winds had unfolded them,
As mine-lamps enkindle a hidden gem,
Shone smiling to heaven, and every one
Shared joy in the light of the gentle sun;

For each one was interpenetrated
With the light and the odor its neighbor shed,
Like young lovers, whom youth and love make dear,
Wrapped and filled by their mutual atmosphere.

But the Sensitive Plant, which could give small fruit
Of the love which it felt from the leaf to the root,
Received more than all, it loved more than ever,
Where none wanted but it, could belong to the giver.

For the Sensitive Plant has no bright flower;
Radiance and odor are not its dower;
It loves, even like Love; its deep heart is full;
It desires what it has not—the beautiful !

The light winds which, from unsustaining
    wings,
Shed the music of many murmurings;
The beams which dart from many a star
Of the flowers whose hues they bear afar;—

The plumed insects, swift and free,
Like golden boats on a sunny sea,
Laden with light and odor, which pass
Over the gleam of the living grass;—

The unseen clouds of the dew, which lie
Like fire in the flowers till the sun rides
    high,
Then wander like spirits among the spheres,
Each cloud faint with the fragrance it
    bears;—

The quivering vapors of dim noon-tide,
Which, like a sea, o'er the warm earth glide,
In which every sound, and odor, and beam,
Move as reeds in a single stream;—

Each and all like ministering angels were,
For the Sensitive Plant sweet joy to bear;
Whilst the lagging hours of the day went by,
Like windless clouds o'er a tender sky.

And when evening descended from heaven above,
And the earth was all rest, and the air was all love,
And delight, though less bright, was far more deep,
And the day's veil fell from the world of sleep;

And the beasts and the birds and the insects were drowned
In an ocean of dreams without a sound;
Whose waves never mark, though they ever impress,
The light sand which paves it—consciousness.

Only overhead the sweet nightingale
Ever sang more sweet as the day might fail,
And snatches of its Elysian chant
Were mixed with the dreams of the Sensitive Plant;

The Sensitive Plant was the earliest
Upgathered into the bosom of rest—
A sweet child, weary of its delight,
The feeblest, and yet the favorite,
Cradled within the embrace of night.

PART II.

THERE was a power in that sweet place—
An Eve in this Eden—a ruling grace,
Which to the flowers, did they waken or dream,
Was as God is to the starry scheme.

A lady—the wonder of her kind,
Whose form was upborne by a lovely mind,
Which, dilating, had moulded her mien and motion,
Like a sea-flower unfolded beneath the ocean—

Tended the garden from morn to even;
And the meteors of that sublunar heaven,
Like the lamps of the air when night walks forth,
Laughed round her footsteps up from the earth!

She had no companion of mortal race,
But her tremulous breath and her flushing face
Told, whilst the morn kissed the sleep from her eyes,
That her dreams were less slumber than paradise.

As if some bright spirit for her sweet sake
Had deserted heaven while the stars were awake;
As if yet around her he lingering were,
Though the veil of daylight concealed him from her.

Her step seemed to pity the grass it prest;
You might hear by the heaving of her breast,
That the coming and the going of the wind
Brought pleasure there, and left passion behind.

And wherever her airy footstep trod,
Her trailing hair from the grassy sod
Erased its light vestige, with shadowy sweep,
Like a sunny storm o'er the dark green deep.

I doubt not the flowers of that garden sweet
Rejoiced in the sound of her gentle feet;
I doubt not they felt the spirit that came
From her glowing fingers through all their frame.

She sprinkled bright water from the stream
On those that were faint with the sunny beam;
And out of the cups of the heavy flowers
She emptied the rain of the thunder-showers.

She lifted their heads with her tender hands,
And sustained them with rods and osier bands;
If the flowers had been her own infants, she
Could never have nursed them more tenderly.

And all killing insects and gnawing worms,
And things of obscene and unlovely forms
She bore in a basket of Indian woof
Into the rough woods far aloof—

In a basket of grasses and wild flowers full,
The freshest her gentle hands could pull,
For the poor banished insects, whose intent,
Although they did ill, was innocent.

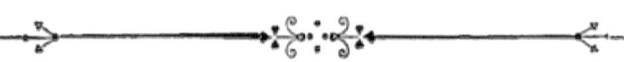

But the bee and the beam-like ephemeris,
Whose path is the lightning's, and the soft moths that kiss
The sweet lips of the flowers, and harm not, did she
Make her attendant angels be.

And many an antenatal tomb,
Where butterflies dream of the life to come,
She left clinging round the smooth and dark
Edge of the odorous cedar bark.

This fairest creature, from earliest spring,
Thus moved through the garden, ministering,
All the sweet season of the summer-tide,
And ere the first leaf looked brown—she died.

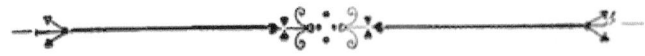

PART III.

THREE days the flowers of the garden fair,
Like stars when the moon is awakened, were;
Or the waves of the Baiæ, ere, luminous,
She floats up through the smoke of Vesuvius.

And on the fourth, the Sensitive Plant
Felt the sound of the funeral chant,
And the steps of the bearers, heavy and slow,
And the sobs of the mourners, deep and low;

The weary sound and the heavy breath,
And the silent motions of passing death,
And the smell, cold, oppressive, and dank,
Sent through the pores of the coffin plank.

The dark grass, and the flowers among the grass,
Were bright with tears as the crowds did pass;
From their sighs the wind caught a mournful tone,
And sate in the pines, and gave groan for groan.

The garden, once fair, became cold and foul,
Like the corpse of her who had been its soul;
Which at first was lovely, as if in sleep,
Then slowly changed, till it grew a heap
To make men tremble who never weep.

Swift summer into the autumn flowed,
And frost in the mist of the morning rode,
Though the noonday sun looked clear and bright,
Mocking the spoil of the secret night.

The rose-leaves, like flakes of crimson snow,
Paved the turf and the moss below;
The Lilies were drooping, and white and wan,
Like the head and skin of a dying man.

And the Indian plants, of scent and hue,
The sweetest that ever were fed on dew,
Leaf after leaf, day by day,
Were massed into the common clay.

And the leaves, brown, yellow, and grey, and red,
And white with the whiteness of what is dead,
Like troops of ghosts on the dry wind passed;
Their whistling noise made the birds aghast.

And the gusty winds waked the winged seeds
Out of their birthplace of ugly weeds,
Till they clung round many a sweet flower's stem,
Which rotted into earth with them.

The water-blooms under the rivulet
Fell from the stalks on which they were set;
And the eddies drove them here and there,
As the winds did those of the upper air.

Then the rain came down, and the broken stalks
Were bent and tangled across the walks;
And the leafless network of parasite bowers
Massed into ruin, and all sweet flowers.

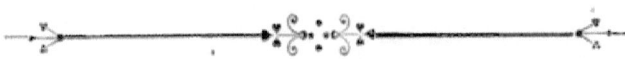

Between the time of the wind and the snow,
All loathliest weeds began to grow,
Whose coarse leaves were splashed with many a speck,
Like the water-snake's belly and the toad's back.

The Sensitive Plant, like one forbid,
Wept, and the tears within each lid
Of its folded leaves which together grew,
Were changed to a blight of frozen glue.

For the leaves soon fell, and the branches soon
By the heavy axe of the blast were hewn;
The sap shrank to the root through every pore,
As blood to a heart that will beat no more.

For winter came: the wind was his whip,
One choppy finger was on his lip;
He had torn the cataracts from the hills,
And they clanked at his girdle like manacles.

His breath was a chain, which, without a sound,
The earth, and the air, and the water bound;
He came, fiercely driven in his chariot throne
By the tenfold blasts of the Arctic zone.

Then the weeds, which were forms of living death,
Fled from the frosts to the earth beneath;
Their decay and sudden flight from frost
Was but like the vanishing of a ghost!

And under the roots of the Sensitive Plant
The moles and the dormice died for want;
And the birds dropped stiff from the frozen air,
And were caught in the branches naked and bare.

First there came down a thawing rain,
And its dull drops froze on the boughs again;
Then there steamed up a freezing dew,
Which to the drops of the thaw-rain grew;

And a northern whirlwind, wandering about
Like a wolf that had smelt a dead child out,
Shook the boughs thus laden and heavy and stiff,
And snapped them off with his rigid griff.

When winter had gone and spring came back,
The Sensitive Plant was a leafless wreck;
But the mandrakes, and toadstools, and docks, and darnels,
Rose, like the dead, from their buried charnels.

CONCLUSION.

WHETHER the Sensitive Plant, or that
Which within its boughs like a spirit sat,
Ere its outward form had known decay,
Now felt this change, I cannot say.

Whether that lady's gentle mind,
No longer with the form combined,
Which scattered love, as stars do light,
Found sadness where it left delight,

I dare not guess; but in this life
Of error, ignorance, and strife,
Where nothing is, but all things seen,
And we the shadows of the dream.

It is a modest creed, and yet
Pleasant, if one considers it,
To own that death itself must be,
Like all the rest, a mockery.

That garden sweet, that lady fair,
And all sweet shapes and odors there,
In truth, have never passed away;
'Tis we, 'tis ours are changed—not they.

For love, and beauty, and delight,
There is no death, nor change; their might
Exceeds our organs, which endure
No light, being themselves obscure.

HORATIUS.

By Thomas Babington Macaulay.

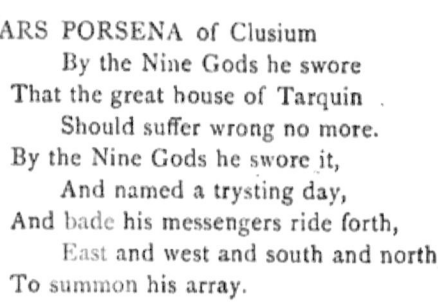

LARS PORSENA of Clusium
  By the Nine Gods he swore
That the great house of Tarquin
  Should suffer wrong no more.
By the Nine Gods he swore it,
  And named a trysting day,
And bade his messengers ride forth,
  East and west and south and north,
To summon his array.

East and west and south and north
  The messengers ride fast,
And tower and town and cottage
  Have heard the trumpet's blast.
Shame on the false Etruscan
  Who lingers in his home
When Porsena of Clusium
  Is on the march for Rome.

The horsemen and the footmen
  Are pouring in amain,
From many a stately market-place;
  From many a fruitful plain;

From many a lonely hamlet,
    Which, hid by beech and pine,
Like an eagle's nest, hangs on the crest
    Of purple Apennine;

From lordly Volaterræ,
    Where scowls the far-famed hold
Piled by the hands of giants
    For godlike kings of old;
From seagirt Populonia,
    Whose sentinels descry
Sardinia's snowy mountain-tops
    Fringing the southern sky;

From the proud mart of Pisæ,
    Queen of the western waves,
Where ride Massilia's triremes
    Heavy with fair-haired slaves;
From where sweet Clanis wanders
    Through corn and vines and flowers;
From where Cortona lifts to heaven
    Her diadem of towers.

Tall are the oaks whose acorns
    Drop in dark Auser's rill;
Fat are the stags that champ the boughs
    Of the Ciminian hill;
Beyond all streams Clitumnus
    Is to the herdsman dear;
Best of all pools for fowler loves
    The great Volsinian mere.

But now no stroke of woodman
    Is heard by Auser's rill;
No hunter tracks the stag's green path
    Up the Ciminian hill;
Unwatched along Clitumnus
    Gazes the milk-white steer;
Unharmed the water-fowl may dip
    In the Volsinian mere.

The harvests of Arretium,
    This year, old men shall reap;
This year, young boys in Umbro
    Shall plunge the struggling sheep;
And in the vats of Luna,
    This year, the must shall foam
Round the white feet of laughing girls,
    Whose sires have marched to Rome.

There be thirty chosen prophets,
    The wisest of the land,
Who alway by Lars Porsena
    Both morn and evening stand:
Evening and morn the Thirty
    Have turned the verses o'er,
Traced from the right on linen white
    By mighty seers of yore.

And with one voice the Thirty
    Have their glad answer given;
"Go forth, go forth, Lars Porsena;
    Go forth, beloved of Heaven;

Go, and return in glory
    To Clusium's royal dome;
And hang round Nurscia's altars
    The golden shields of Rome."

And now hath every city
    Sent up her tale of men;
The foot are fourscore thousand,
    The horse are thousands ten.
Before the gates of Sutrium
    Is met the great array.
A proud man was Lars Porsena
    Upon the trysting day.

For all the Etruscan armies
    Were ranged beneath his eye,
And many a banished Roman
    And many a stout ally;
And with a mighty following
    To join the muster came
The Tusculan Mamilius,
    Prince of the Latin name.

But by the yellow Tiber
    Was tumult and affright:
From all the spacious champaign
    To Rome men took their flight.
A mile around the city,
    The throng stopped up the ways;
A fearful sight it was to see
    Through two long nights and days.

For aged folk on crutches,
    And women great with child,
And mothers sobbing over babes
    That clung to them and smiled,
And sick men borne in litters
    High on the necks of slaves,
And troops of sun-burned husbandmen
    With reaping-hooks and staves.

And droves of mules and asses
    Laden with skins of wine,
And endless flocks of goats and sheep,
    And endless herds of kine,
And endless trains of wagons
    That cracked beneath the weight
Of corn-sacks and of household goods,
    Choked every roaring gate.

Now from the rock Tarpeian,
    Could the wan burghers spy
The line of blazing villages
    Red in the midnight sky.
The Fathers of the City,
    They sat all night and day,
For every hour some horseman came
    With tidings of dismay.

To eastward and to westward
    Have spread the Tuscan bands;
Nor house, nor fence, nor dovecote
    In Crustumerium stands.

Verbenna down to Ostia
   Hath wasted all the plain;
Astur hath stormed Janiculum,
   And the stout guards are slain.

I wis, in all the Senate,
   There was no heart so bold,
But sore it ached, and fast it beat,
   When that ill news was told.
Forthwith up rose the Consul,
   Up rose the Fathers all;
In haste they girded up their gowns,
   And hied them to the wall.

They held a council standing
   Before the River-gate;
Short time was there, ye well may guess,
   For musing or debate.
Out spake the Consul roundly:
   " The bridge must straight go down;
For, since Janiculum is lost,
   Naught else can save the town.

Just then a scout came flying,
   All wild with haste and fear:
" To arms ! to arms ! Sir Consul;
   Lars Porsena is here."
On the low hills to westward
   The Consul fixed his eye,
And saw the swarthy storm of dust
   Rise fast along the sky.

And nearer fast and nearer
 Doth the red whirlwind come;
And louder still, and still more loud
From underneath that rolling cloud,
Is heard the trumpet's war-note proud.
 The trampling, and the hum.
And plainly and more plainly
 Now through the gloom appears,
Far to the left and far to the right,
In broken gleams of dark-blue light,
The long array of helmets bright,
 The long array of spears.

And plainly and more plainly,
 Above that glimmering line,
Now might ye see the banners
 Of twelve fair cities shine;
But the banner of proud Clusium
 Was highest of them all,
The terror of the Umbrian,
 The terror of the Gaul.

And plainly and more plainly
 Now might the burghers know,
By port and vest, by horse and crest,
 Each warlike Lucomo.
There Cilnius of Arretium
 On his fleet roan was seen;
And Astur of the four-fold shield,
Girt with the brand none else may wield,
Tolumnius with the belt of gold,
And dark Verbenna from the hold
 By reedy Thrasymene.

Fast by the royal standard,
    O'erlooking all the war,
Lars Porsena of Clusium
    Sat in his ivory car.
By the right wheel rode Mamilius,
    Prince of the Latin name;
And by the left false Sextus,
    That wrought the deed of shame.

But when the face of Sextus
    Was seen among the foes
A yell that rent the firmament
    From all the town arose.
On the house-tops was no woman
    But spat towards him and hissed;
No child but screamed out curses,
    And shook its little fist.

But the Consul's brow was sad,
    And the Consul's speech was low,
And darkly looked he at the wall,
    And darkly at the foe.
"Their van will be upon us
    Before the bridge goes down;
And if they once may win the bridge,
    What hope to save the town?"

Then out spake brave Horatius,
    The Captain of the gate:
"To every man upon this earth
    Death cometh soon or late.

And how can man die better
    Than facing fearful odds,
For the ashes of his fathers
    And the temples of his Gods,

" And for the tender mother
    Who dandled him to rest,
And for the wife who nurses
    His baby at her breast,
And for the holy maidens
    Who feed the eternal flame,
To save them from false Sextus
    That wrought the deed of shame?

" Hew down the bridge, Sir Consul,
    With all the speed ye may;
I, with two more to help me,
    Will hold the foe in play.
In yon strait path a thousand
    May well be stopped by three.
Now who will stand on either hand,
    And keep the bridge with me?"

Then out spake Spurius Lartius
    A Ramnian proud was he:
" Lo, I will stand at thy right hand,
    And keep the bridge with thee."
And out spake strong Herminius;
    Of Titian blood was he:
" I will abide on thy left side,
    And keep the bridge with thee."

" Horatius," quoth the Consul,
    "As thou sayest, so let it be."
And straight against that great array
    Forth went the dauntless Three.
For Romans in Rome's quarrel
    Spared neither land nor gold,
Nor son nor wife, nor limb nor life,
    In the brave days of old.

Then none was for a party;
    Then all were for the state:
Then the great man helped the poor,
    And the poor man loved the great:
Then lands were fairly portioned:
    Then spoils were fairly sold:
The Romans were like brothers
    In the brave days of old.

Now Roman is to Roman,
    More hateful than a foe,
And the Tribunes beard the high,
    And the Fathers grind the low.
As we wax hot in faction,
    In battle we wax cold:
Wherefore men fight not as they fought
    In the brave days of old.

Now while the Three were tightening
    Their harness on their backs,
The Consul was the foremost man
    To take in hand an axe:

And Fathers mixed with Commons
    Seized hatchet, bar, and crow,
And smote upon the planks above,
    And loosed the props below.

Meanwhile the Tuscan army,
    Right glorious to behold,
Came flashing back the noonday light,
Rank behind rank, like surges bright.
    Of a broad sea of gold.
Four hundred trumpets sounded
    A peal of warlike glee,
As that great host, with measured tread,
And spears advanced, and ensigns spread,
Rolled slowly towards the bridge's head,
    Where stood the dauntless Three.

The Three stood calm and silent
    And looked upon the foes,
And a great shout of laughter
    From all the vanguard rose:
And forth three chiefs came spurring
    Before that deep array;
To earth they sprang, their swords they drew
And lifted high their shields, and flew
    To win the narrow way;

Aunus from green Tifernum,
    Lord of the Hill of Vines;
And Seius, whose eight hundred slaves
    Sicken in Ilva's mines;

And Picus, long to Clusium
    Vassal in peace and war,
Who led to fight his Umbrian powers
From that gray crag where, girt with towers,
The fortress of Nequinum lowers
    O'er the pale waves of Nar.

Stout Lartius hurled down Aunus
    Into the stream beneath:
Herminius struck at Seius,
    And clove him to the teeth:
At Picus brave Horatius
    Darted one fiery thrust;
And the proud Umbrian's gilded arms
    Clashed in the bloody dust.

Then Ocnus of Falerii
    Rushed on the Roman Three;
And Lausulus of Urgo,
    The rover of the sea;
And Aruns of Volsinium,
    Who slew the great wild boar,
The great wild boar that had his den
Amidst the reeds of Cosa's fen,
And wasted fields, and slaughtered men,
    Along Albinia's shore.

Herminius smote down Aruns:
    Lartius laid Ocnus low:
Right to the heart of Lausulus
    Horatius sent a blow.

"Lie there," he cried, "fell pirate!
    No more, aghast and pale,
From Ostia's walls the crowd shall mark
The track of thy destroying bark.
No more Campania's hinds shall fly
To woods and caverns when they spy
    Thy thrice accursed sail."

But now no sound of laughter
    Was heard among the foes.
A wild and wrathful clamour
    From all the vanguard rose.
Six spears' lengths from the entrance
    Halted that deep array,
And for a space no man came forth
    To win the narrow way.

But hark! the cry is Astur:
    And lo! the ranks divide;
And the great Lord of Luna
    Comes with his stately stride.
Upon his ample shoulders
    Clangs loud the four-fold shield.
And in his hand he shakes the brand
    Which none but he can wield.

He smiled on those bold Romans
    A smile serene and high;
He eyed the flinching Tuscans,
    And scorn was in his eye.

Quoth he, " The she-wolf's litter
 Stand savagely at bay:
But will ye dare to follow,
 If Astur clears the way ? "

Then, whirling up his broadsword
 With both hands to the height,
He rushed against Horatius,
 And smote with all his might.
With shield and blade Horatius
 Right deftly turned the blow.
The blow, though turned, came yet too nigh;
It missed his helm, but gashed his thigh:
The Tuscans raised a joyful cry
 To see the red blood flow.

He reeled, and on Herminius
 He leaned one breathing-space;
Then, like a wild cat mad with wounds,
 Sprang right at Astur's face.
Through teeth, and skull, and helmet,
 So fierce a thrust he sped,
The good sword stood a hand-breadth out
 Behind the Tuscan's head.

And the great Lord of Luna
 Fell at that deadly stroke,
As falls on Mount Alvernus
 A thunder-smitten oak.

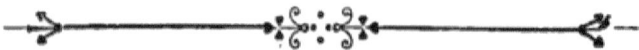

Far o'er the crashing forest
    The giant arms lie spread:
And the pale augurs, muttering low,
    Gaze on the blasted head.

On Astur's throat Horatius
    Right firmly pressed his heel,
And thrice and four times tugged amain
    Ere he wrenched out the steel.
"And see," he cried, "the welcome
    Fair guests, that waits you here !
What noble Lucomo comes next,
    To taste our Roman cheer ? "

But at this haughty challenge
    A sullen murmur ran,
Mingled of wrath, and shame, and dread,
    Along that glittering van.
There lacked not men of prowess,
    Nor men of lordly race;
For all Etruria's noblest
    Were round the fatal place.

But all Etruria's noblest
    Felt their hearts sink to see
On the earth the bloody corpses,
    In the path the dauntless Three;
And, from the ghastly entrance
    Where those bold Romans stood,
All shrank, like boys who unaware,

Ranging the woods to start a hare,
Come to the mouth of the dark lair
Where, growling low, a fierce old bear
  Lies amidst bones and blood.

Was none who would be foremost
    To lead such dire attack;
But those behind cried " Forward ! "
    And those before cried " Back ! "
And backward now and forward
    Wavers the deep array;
And on the tossing sea of steel,
To and fro the standards reel;
And the victorious trumpet's peal
    Dies fitfully away.

Yet one man for one moment
    Strode out before the crowd;
Well known was he to all the Three,
    As they gave him greeting loud.
" Now welcome, welcome Sextus !
    Now welcome to thy home !
Why dost thou stay, and turn away ?
    Here lies the road to Rome."

Thrice looked he at the city;
    Thrice looked he at the dead;
And thrice came on in fury,
    And thrice turned back in dread:

And, white with fear and hatred,
    Scowled at the narrow way
Where, wallowing in a pool of blood,
    The bravest Tuscans lay.

But meanwhile axe and lever
    Have manfully been plied,
And now the bridge hangs tottering
    Above the boiling tide.
"Come back, come back, Horatius!"
    Loud cried the Fathers all.
"Back, Lartius! back, Herminius!
    Back, ere the ruin fall!"

Back darted Spurius Lartius;
    Herminius darted back:
And, as they passed, beneath their feet
    They felt the timbers crack.
But when they turned their faces,
    And on the farther shore
Saw brave Horatius stand alone,
    They would have crossed once more;

But with a crash like thunder
    Fell every loosened beam,
And, like a dam, the mighty wreck
    Lay right athwart the stream;
And a long shout of triumph
    Rose from the walls of Rome,
As to the highest turret-tops
    Was splashed the yellow foam.

And, like a horse unbroken
    When first he feels the rein,
The furious river struggled hard,
    And tossed his tawny mane,
And burst the curb, and bounded,
    Rejoicing to be free,
And whirling down, in fierce career
Battlement, and plank, and pier,
    Rushed headlong to the sea.

Alone stood brave Horatius,
    But constant still in mind;
Thrice thirty thousand foes before,
    And the broad flood behind.
"Down with him!" cried false Sextus,
    With a smile on his pale face.
"Now yield thee," cried Lars Porsena,
    "Now yield thee to our grace."

Round turned he, as not deigning
    Those craven ranks to see;
Naught spake he to Lars Porsena,
    To Sextus naught spake he:
But he saw on Palatinus
    The white porch of his home;
And he spake to the noble river
    That rolls by the towers of Rome.

"Oh, Tiber! Father Tiber!
    To whom the Romans pray,
A Roman's life, a Roman's arms,
    Take thou in charge this day!"

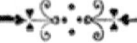

So he spake, and speaking sheathed
    The good sword by his side,
And with his harness on his back,
    Plunged headlong in the tide.

No sound of joy or sorrow
    Was heard from either bank;
But friends and foes in dumb surprise,
With parted lips and straining eyes,
    Stood gazing where he sank;
And when above the surges
    They saw his crest appear,
All Rome sent forth a rapturous cry,
And even the ranks of Tuscany
    Could scarce forbear to cheer.

But fiercely ran the current,
    Swollen high by months of rain:
And fast his blood was flowing;
    And he was sore in pain,
And heavy with his armour,
    And spent with changing blows:
And oft they thought him sinking,
    But still again he rose.

Never, I ween, did swimmer,
    In such an evil case,
Struggle through such a raging flood
    Safe to the landing-place:
But his limbs were borne up bravely
    By the brave heart within,
And our good Father Tiber
    Bare bravely up his chin.

"Curse on him!" quoth false Sextus:
     "Will not the villain drown?
But for this stay, ere close of day
     We should have sacked the town!"
"Heaven help him!" quoth Lars Porsena,
     "And bring him safe to shore:
For such a gallant feat of arms
     Was never seen before."

And now he feels the bottom;
     Now on dry earth he stands;
Now round him throng the Fathers
     To press his gory hands; .
And now, with shouts and clapping,
     And noise of weeping loud,
He enters through the River-Gate
     Borne by the joyous crowd.

They gave him of the corn-land
     That was of public right
As much as two strong oxen
     Could plough from morn till night;
And they made a molten image,
     And set it up on high,
And there it stands unto this day
     To witness if I lie.

It stands in the Comitium,
     Plain for all folk to see;
Horatius in his harness,
     Halting upon one knee:

And underneath is written,
      In letters all of gold,
How valiantly he kept the bridge
      In the brave days of old.

And still his name sounds stirring
      Unto the men of Rome,
As the trumpet-blast that cries to them
      To charge the Volscian home;
And wives still pray to Juno
      For boys with hearts as bold
As his who kept the bridge so well
      In the brave days of old.

And in the nights of winter,
      When the cold north winds blow,
And the long howling of the wolves
      Is heard amidst the snow;
When round the lonely cottage
      Roars loud the tempest's din;
And the good logs of Algidus
      Roar louder yet within;

When the oldest cask is opened,
      And the largest lamp is lit;
When the chestnuts glow in the embers,
      And the kid turns on the spit;
When young and old in circle
      Around the firebrands close;
When the girls are weaving baskets,
      And the lads are shaping bows;

When the goodman mends his armour,
    And trims his helmet's plume;
When the goodwife's shuttle merrily
    Goes flashing through the loom;
With weeping and with laughter
    Still is the story told,
How well Horatius kept the bridge
    In the brave days of old.

➤❋THE✛CHANGED✛CROSS.❋◄

By Hon. Mrs. Charles Hobart.

'T was a time of sadness, and my heart,
Although it knew and loved the better part,
Felt wearied with the conflict and the strife,
And all the needful discipline of life.

And while I thought on these, as given to me—
My trial tests of faith and love to be—
It seemed as if I never could be sure
That faithful to the end I should endure.

And thus, no longer trusting to His might
Who says, "We walk by faith, and not by sight,"
Doubting, and almost yielding to despair,
The thought arose—My cross I cannot bear:

Far heavier its weight must surely be
Than those of others which I daily see.
Oh! if I might another burden choose,
Methinks I should not fear my crown to lose.

A solemn silence reigned on all around—
E'en Nature's voices uttered not a sound;
The evening shadows seemed of peace to tell,
And sleep upon my weary spirit fell.

A moment's pause—and then a heavenly light
Beamed full upon my wondering, raptured sight;
Angels on silvery wings seemed everywhere,
And angels' music thrilled the balmy air.

Then One, more fair than all the rest to see—
One to whom all the others bowed the knee—
Came gently to me as I trembling lay,
And "Follow me!" He said; "I am the Way."

Then, speaking thus, He led me far above,
And there, beneath a canopy of love,
Crosses of divers shape and size were seen,
Larger and smaller than my own had been.

And one there was, most beauteous to behold,
A little one, with jewels set in gold.
Ah! this, methought, I can with comfort wear,
For it will be an easy one to bear:

And so the little cross I quickly took;
But, all at once, my frame beneath it shook.
The sparkling jewels fair were they to see,
But far too heavy was their *weight* for me.

"This may not be," I cried, and looked again,
To see if there was any here could ease my pain;
But, one by one, I passed them slowly by,
Till on a lovely one I cast my eye.

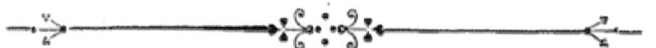

Fair flowers around its sculptured form entwined,
And grace and beauty seemed in it combined,
Wondering, I gazed; and still I wondered more
To think so many should have passed it o'er.

But oh ! that form so beautiful to see
Soon made its hidden sorrows known to me;
Thorns lay beneath those flowers and colors fair !
Sorrowing, I said: "This cross I may not bear."

And so it was with each and all around—
Not one to suit my *need* could there be found;
Weeping, I laid each heavy burden down,
As my Guide gently said: "No cross, no crown."

At length, to Him I raised my saddened heart:
He knew its sorrows, bid its doubts depart.
" Be not afraid," He said, " but trust in me—
My perfect love shall now be shown to thee."

And then, with lightened eyes and willing feet,
Again I turned, my earthly cross to meet,
With forward footsteps, turning not aside,
For fear some hidden evil might betide;

And there—in the prepared, appointed way,
Listening to hear, and ready to obey—
A cross I quickly found of plainest form,
With only words of love inscribed thereon.

With thankfulness I raised it from the rest,
And joyfully acknowledged it the best—
The only one of all the many there
That I could feel was good for me to bear.

And, while I thus my chosen one confess
I saw a heavenly brightness on it rest;
And, as I bent, my burden to sustain,
I recognized my own old cross again.

But oh ! how different did it seem to be
Now I had learned its preciousness to see !
No longer could I unbelieving say,
Perhaps another is a better way.

Ah no ! henceforth my own desire shall be,
That He who knows me best should choose for me,
And so, whate'er His love sees good to send,
I'll trust it's best, because He knows the end.

➤❋THE✚BURIAL✚OF✚MOSES.❋⬅

By Mrs. C. F. Alexander.

B Y Nebo's lonely mountain,
  On this side Jordan's wave,
In a vale in the land of Moab,
  There lies a lonely grave;
And no man dug that sepulchre,
  And no man saw it e'er,
For the "Sons of God" upturned the sod,
  And laid the dead man there.

That was the grandest funeral
  That ever passed on earth;
But no man heard the trampling,
  Or saw the train go forth.
Noiselessly as the day-light
  Comes when the night is done,
And the crimson streak on ocean's cheek
  Grows into the great sun—

Noiselessly as the spring-time
  Her crown of verdure weaves
And all the trees on all the hills
  Open their thousand leaves;
So, without sound of music,
  Or voice of them that wept,
Silently down from the mountain's crown
  The great procession swept.

Perchance the bald old eagle,
　　On gray Beth-peor's height,
Out of his rocky eyry
　　Looked on the wondrous sight;
Perchance the lion stalking
　　Still shuns that hallowed spot:
For beast and bird have seen and heard
　　That which man knoweth not.

But when the warrior dieth,
　　His comrades in the war,
With arms reversed, and muffled drum,
　　Follow the funeral car.
They show the banners taken,
　　They tell his battles won,
And after him lead his masterless steed,
　　While peals the minute-gun.

Amid the noblest of the land
　　Men lay the sage to rest,
And give the bard an honored place,
　　With costly marble drest—
In the great minster transept,
　　Where lights like glories fall,
And the sweet choir sings, and the organ rings
　　Along the emblazoned wall.

This was the bravest warrior
　　That ever buckled sword;
This, the most gifted poet
　　That ever breathed a word;

And never earth's philosopher
  Traced with his golden pen,
On the deathless page, truths half so sage
  As he wrote down for men.

And had he not high honor?
  The hill-side for his pall,
To lie in state while angels wait,
  With stars for tapers tall,
And the dark rock-pines like tossing plumes
  Over his bier to wave,
And God's own hand, in that lonely land,
  To lay him in the grave!

In that deep grave without a name,
  Whence his uncoffined clay
Shall break again—most wondrous thought—
  Before the Judgment day,
And stand, with glory wrapped around,
  On the hills he never trod,
And speak of the strife that won our life
  With the Incarnate Son of God.

O lonely tomb in Moab's land!
  O dark Beth-peor hill!
Speak to these curious hearts of ours,
  And teach them to be still.
God hath His mysteries of grace,
  Ways that we cannot tell;
And hides them deep, like the secret sleep
  Of him He loved so well.

→✳SONG.✳←

BY SIR WALTER SCOTT.

HERE shall the lover rest,
  Whom the Fates sever,
From his true maiden's breast
  Parted for ever?
Where, through groves deep and high
  Sounds the far billow,
Where early violets die,
  Under the willow.

There through the summer day,
  Cool streams are laving;
There, while the tempests sway,
  Scarce are boughs waving;
There, thy rest shalt thou take,
  Parted for ever,
Never again to wake,
  Never, O never.

Where shall the traitor rest,
  He, the deceiver,
Who could win maiden's breast,
  Ruin, and leave her?

" There through the summer day,
Cool streams are laving."

In the lost battle,
    Borne down by the flying,
Where mingles war's rattles
    With groans of the dying.

Her wing shall the eagle flap
    O'er the false-hearted;
His warm blood the wolf shall lap,
    Ere life be parted.
Shame and dishonor sit
    By his grave ever;
Blessing shall hallow it,—
   ' Never, O never.

➤✳NATURELLE.✳⬅

MY goddess romped at school,
　　Fetched April's boldest violet;
　Her crown was her brown hair
　　With diamonds of its own gloss set.

I envied not the Greek;
　　Callisto, Io, Proserpine,
From all their ills were saved
　　Had Reus and Dis her beauty seen.

Fine dames forgot their airs,
　　And when her step led through the mart
Traffic forebore its greed;
　　Yet simpleness was all her art.

For beauty use her rule,
　　Her language, tone, and gentle ways;
Her grace showed best in tasks
　　She loved; and peace filled all the days.

A maid, when last we met,
　　A woman's form is now her earthly dress;
O Time and World, I pray,
　　Ye have not changed her simpleness!

➤THE✦MOTHER'S✦HEART.✦◄

BY CAROLINE·E. NORTON.

HEN first thou camest, gently, shy, and fond,
　　My eldest born, first hope, and dearest
　　treasure,
My heart received thee with a joy beyond
　　All that it yet had felt of earthly pleasure;
Nor thought that any love again might be
So deep and strong as that I felt for thee.

Faithful and true, with sense beyond thy years,
　　And natural piety that leaned to heaven;
Wrung by a harsh word suddenly to tears,
　　Yet patient to rebuke when justly given;
Obedient, easy to be reconciled,
And meekly cheerful; such wert thou, my child !

Not willing to be left—still by my side,
　　Haunting my walks, while summer-day was dying;
Nor leaving in thy turn, but pleased to glide
　　Through the dark room where I was sadly lying;
Or by the couch of pain, a sitter meek,
Watch the dim eye, and kiss the fevered cheek.

O boy! of such as thou are oftenest made
    Earth's fragile idols; like a tender flower,
No strength in all thy freshness, prone to fade,
    And bending weakly to the thunder-shower;
Still, round the loved, thy heart found force to bind, ·
And clung, like woodbine shaken in the wind!

Then THOU, my merry love,—bold in thy glee,
    Under the bough, or by the firelight dancing,
With thy sweet temper, and thy spirit free,—
    Didst come, as restless as a bird's wing glancing,
Full of a wild and irrepressible mirth,
Like a young sunbeam to the gladdened earth!

Thine was the shout, the song, the burst of joy,
    Which sweet from childhood's rosy lip resoundeth;
Thine was the eager spirit naught could cloy,
    And the glad heart from which all grief reboundeth;
And many a mirthful jest and mock reply
Lurked in the laughter of thy dark-blue eye.

And thine was many an art to win and bless,
    The cold and stern to joy and fondness warming;
The coaxing smile, the frequent soft caress,
    The earnest, tearful prayer all wrath disarming!
Again my heart a new affection found,
But thought that love with thee had reached its bound.

At length THOU camest,—thou, the last and least,
    Nicknamed "the Emperor" by thy laughing brothers,
Because a haughty spirit swelled thy breast,
    And thou didst seek to rule and sway the others,
Mingling with every playful infant wile
A mimic majesty that made us smile.

And O, most like a regal child wert thou !
 An eye of resolute and successful scheming !
Fair shoulders, curling lips, and dauntless brow,
 Fit for the world's strife, not for poet's dreaming;
And proud the lifting of thy stately head,
And the firm bearing of thy conscious tread.

Different from both ! yet each succeeding claim
 I, that all other love had been forswearing,
Forthwith admitted, equal and the same;
 Nor injured either by this love's comparing,
Nor stole a fraction for the newer call,—
But in the mother's heart found room for all !

⇒❊LITTLE✧BILLEE.❊⇐

BY WILLIAM MAKEPEACE THACKERAY.

THERE were three sailors of Bristol City
    Who took a boat and went to sea,
But first with beef and captain's biscuits
    And pickled pork they loaded she.

There was gorging Jack, and guzzling Jimmy,
    And the youngest he was little Billee;
Now when they 'd got as far as the Equator
    They 'd nothing left but one split pea.

Says gorging Jack to guzzling Jimmy,
    "I am extremely hungaree."
To gorging Jack says guzzling Jimmy,
    "We 've nothing left, us must eat we."

Says gorging Jack to guzzling Jimmy,
    "With one another we should n't agree!
There 's little Bill, he 's young and tender,
    We 're old and tough, so let 's eat he."

"O Billy! we 're going to kill and eat you,
    So undo the button of your chemie."
When Bill received this information,
    He used his pocket-handkerchie.

" First let me say my catechism
    Which my poor mother taught to me."
" Make haste ! make haste !" says guzzling Jimmy,
    While Jack pulled out his snickersnee.

Billy went up the main-top-gallant mast,
    And down he fell on his bended knee,
He scarce had come to the Twelfth Commandment
    When he jumps up—"There's land I see !"

" Jerusalem and Madagascar
    And North and South Amerikee,
There's the British flag a-riding at anchor,
    With Admiral Napier, K. C. B."

So when they got aboard of the Admiral's,
    He hanged fat Jack and flogged Jimmee,
But as for little Bill he made him
    The Captain of a Seventy-three.

→*THE✢VAGABONDS.*←

By J. T. Trowbridge.

E are two travelers, Roger and I.
    Roger's my dog:—come here, you scamp!
Jump for the gentlemen,—mind your eye!
    Over the table,—look out for the lamp!—
The rogue is growing a little old;
    Five years we've tramped through wind and
        weather,
And slept out-doors when nights were cold,
    And ate and drank—and starved together.

We've learned what comfort is, I tell you!
    A bed on the floor, a bit of rosin,
A fire to thaw our thumbs, (poor fellow!
    The paw he holds up there's been frozen,)
Plenty of catgut for my fiddle,
    (This out-door business is bad for strings,)
Then a few nice buckwheats hot from the griddle,
    And Roger and I set up for kings!

No, thank ye, sir,—I never drink;
    Roger and I are exceedingly moral,—
Aren't we, Roger?— see him wink!—
    Well, something hot, then,—we won't quarrel.
He's thirsty, too,—see him nod his head?
    What a pity, sir, that dogs can't talk!
He understands every word that's said,—
    And he knows good milk from water-and-chalk.

The truth is, sir, now I reflect,
    I've been so sadly given to grog,
I wonder I've not lost the respect
    (Here's to you, sir!) even of my dog.
But he sticks by, through thick and thin;
    And this old coat, with its empty pockets,
And rags that smell of tobacco and gin,
    He'll follow while he has eyes in his sockets.

There isn't another creature living
    Would do it, and prove, through every disaster,
So fond, so faithful, and so forgiving,
    To such a miserable, thankless master!
No, sir!—see him wag his tail and grin!
    By George! it makes my old eyes water!
That is, there's something in this gin
    That chokes a fellow.   But no matter!

We'll have some music, if you're willing,
    And Roger (hem! what a plague a cough is, sir!)
Shall march a little.—Start, you villain!
    Stand straight! 'Bout face! Salute your officer!
Put up that paw! Dress! Take your rifle!
    (Some dogs have arms, you see!) Now hold your
Cap while the gentlemen give a trifle,
    To aid a poor old patriot soldier!

March! Halt! Now show how the rebel shakes,
    When he stands up to hear his sentence.
Now tell us how many drams it takes
    To honor a jolly new acquaintance.
Five yelps,—that's five; he's mighty knowing!
    The night's before us, fill the glasses!—
Quick, sir! I'm ill,—my brain is going!—
    Some brandy!—thank you!—there!—it passes!

Why not reform ?   That's easily said;
  But I've gone through such wretched treatment,
Sometimes forgetting the taste of bread,
  And scarce remembering what meat meant,
That my poor stomach's past reform;
  And there are times when, mad with thinking,
I'd sell out heaven for something warm
  To prop a horrible inward sinking.

Is there a way to forget to think ? ·
  At your age, sir, home, fortune, friends,
A dear girl's love,—but I took to drink;—
  The same old story; you know how it ends.
If you could have seen these classic features,—
  You needn't laugh, sir; they were not then
Such a burning libel on God's creatures:
  I was one of your handsome men !

If you had seen her, so fair and young,
  Whose head was happy on this breast !
If you could have heard the songs I sung
  When the wine went round, you wouldn't have guessed
That ever I, sir, should be straying
  From door to door, with fiddle and dog,
Ragged and penniless, and playing
  To you to-night for a glass of grog !

She's married since,—a parson's wife :
  'Twas better for her that we should part,—
Better the soberest, prosiest life
  Than a blasted home and a broken heart.
I have seen her ? Once : I was weak and spent
  On the dusty road, a carriage stopped :
But little she dreamed, as on she went,
  Who kissed the coin that her fingers dropped !

You've set me talking, sir ; I'm sorry ;
    It makes me wild to think of the change !
What do you care for a beggar's story ?
    Is it amusing ? you find it strange.
I had a mother so proud of me !
    'Twas well she died before—— Do you know
If the happy spirits in heaven can see
    The ruin and wretchedness here below ?

Another glass, and strong, to deaden
    This pain; then Roger and I will start
I wonder, has he such a lumpish, leaden,
    Aching thing, in place of a heart?
He is sad sometimes, and would weep, if he could,
    No doubt, remembering things that were,—
A virtuous kennel, with plenty of food,
    And himself a sober, respectable cur.

I'm better now; that glass was warming,—
    You rascal ! limber your lazy feet !
We must be fiddling and performing
    For supper and bed, or starve in the street.—
Not a very gay life to lead, you think ?
    But soon we shall go where lodgings are free,
And the sleepers need neither victuals nor drink;—
    The sooner, the better for Roger and me !

THE PARTING HOUR.

BY EDWARD POLLOCK.

[The following exquisite poem was written by the late Edward Pollock, the gifted Californian poet, on the 6th January, 1857, and has never been published. It was given by the poet to a friend who was about to depart on a steamer for Oregon, Pollock saying, "Take this; you may perhaps read and appreciate the sentiment long after I have ceased to be among the living."]

THERE'S something in the "parting hour"
    Will chill the warmest heart—
Yet kindred, comrades, lovers, friends,
    Are fated all to part;
But this I've seen—and many a page
    Has pressed it on my mind—
The one who goes is happier
    Than those he leaves behind.

No matter what the journey be,
    Adventurous, dangerous, far,
To the wild deep or black frontier,
    To solitude or war—
Still something cheers the heart that dares
    In all of human kind,
And they who go are happier
    Than those they leave behind.

The bride goes to the bridegroom's home
  With doubtings and with tears.
But does not hope her rainbow spread
  Across her cloudy fears?
Alas! the mother who remains,
  What comfort can she find,
But this—the gone is happier
  Than one she leaves behind.

Have you a friend—a comrade dear—
  An old and valued friend?
Be sure your term of sweet concourse
  At length will have an end.
And when you part—as part you will—
  O take it not unkind
If he who goes is happier
  Than you he leaves behind!

God wills it so—and so it is;
  The pilgrims on their way,
Though weak and worn, more cheerful are
  Than all the rest who stay;
And when, at last, poor man, subdued,
  Lies down to death resigned,
May he not still be happier far
  Than those he leaves behind?

➤❋THE✦ORIENT❋◄

FROM THE "BRIDE OF ABYDOS."

BY BYRON.

NOW ye the land where the cypress and myrtle
    Are emblems of deeds that are done in their
       clime,
    Where the rage of the vulture, the love of the
       turtle,
      Now melt into sorrow, now madden to crime?
Know ye the land of the cedar and vine,
Where the flowers ever blossom, the beams ever shine:
Where the light wings of Zephyr, oppressed with perfume,
Wax faint o'er the gardens of Gul in her bloom !
Where the citron and olive are fairest of fruit,
And the voice of the nightingale never is mute,
Where the tints of the earth, and the hues of the sky,
In color though varied, in beauty may vie,
And the purple of ocean is deepest in dye;
Where the virgins are soft as the roses they twine,
And all, save the spirit of man, is divine ?
'T is the clime of the East; 't is the land of the Sun,—
Can he smile on such deeds as his children have done ?
O, wild as the accents of lover's farewell
Are the hearts which they bear and the tales which they tell !

" Where the flowers ever blossom, the beams ever shine."

CURFEW MUST NOT RING TO-NIGHT

NGLAND'S sun was slowly setting
    O'er the hills so far away,
Filling all the land with beauty
    At the close of one sad day;
And the last rays kiss'd the forehead
    Of a man and maiden fair,
He with step so slow and weakened,
    She with sunny, floating hair;
He with sad bowed head, and thoughtful,
    She with lips so cold and white,
Struggling to keep back the murmur,
    "Curfew must not ring to-night."

"Sexton," Bessie's white lips faltered,
    Pointing to the prison old,
With its walls so dark and gloomy,—
    Walls so dark, and damp, and cold,—
"I've a lover in that prison,
    Doomed this very night to die,
At the ringing of the Curfew,
    And no earthly help is nigh.
Cromwell will not come till sunset,"
    And her face grew strangely white,
As she spoke in husky whispers,
    "Curfew must not ring to-night."

" Bessie," calmly spoke the Sexton—
    Every word pierced her young heart
Like a thousand gleaming arrows—
    Like a deadly poisoned dart;
" Long, long years I've rung the Curfew
    From that gloomy shadowed tower;
Every evening, just at sunset,
    It has told the twilight hour;
I have done my duty ever,
    Tried to do it just and right,
Now I'm old, I will not miss it;
    Girl, the Curfew rings to-night!"

Wild her eyes and pale her features,
    Stern and white her thoughtful brow,
And within her heart's deep centre,
    Bessie made a solemn vow;
She had listened while the judges
    Read, without a tear or sigh,
" At the ringing of the Curfew—
    Basil Underwood *must die*."
And her breath came fast and faster,
    And her eyes grew large and bright—
One low murmur, scarcely spoken—
    " Curfew *must not* ring to-night!"

She with light step bounded forward,
    Sprang within the old church door,
Left the old man coming slowly,
    Paths he'd often trod before,
Not one moment paused the maiden,
    But with cheek and brow aglow,

Staggered up the gloomy tower,
    Where the bell swung to and fro:
Then she climbed the slimy ladder,
    Dark, without one ray of light,
Upward still, her pale lips saying:
    "Curfew shall not ring to-night."

She has reached the topmost ladder,
    O'er her hangs the great dark bell.
And the awful gloom beneath her,
    Like the pathway down to hell;
See, the ponderous tongue is swinging,
    'Tis the hour of Curfew now—
And the sight has chilled her bosom,
    Stopped her breath and paled her brow.
Shall she let it ring?   No, never!
    Her eyes flash with sudden light,
As she springs and grasps it firmly—
    "Curfew shall not ring to-night!"

Out she swung, far out, the city
    Seemed a tiny speck below;
There, 'twixt heaven and earth suspended,
    As the bell swung to and fro;
And the half-deaf Sexton ringing
    (Years he had not heard the bell,)
And he thought the twilight Curfew
    Rang young Basil's funeral knell;
Still the maiden clinging firmly,
    Cheek and brow so pale and white,
Stilled her frightened heart's wild beating—
    "Curfew shall not ring to-night."

It was o'er—the bell ceased swaying,
   And the maiden stepped once more
Firmly on the damp old ladder,
   Where for hundred years before
Human foot had not been planted;
   And what she this night had done,
Should be told in long years after—
   As the rays of setting sun
Light the sky with mellow beauty,
   Aged sires with heads of white,
Tell the children why the Curfew
   Did not ring that one sad night.

O'er the distant hills came Cromwell;
   Bessie saw him, and her brow,
Lately white with sickening terror,
   Glows with sudden beauty now;
At his feet she told her story,
   Showed her hands all bruised and torn;
And her sweet young face so haggard,
   With a look so sad and worn,
Touched his heart with sudden pity—
   Lit his eyes with misty light;
"Go, your lover lives!" cried Cromwell;
   "Curfew shall not ring to-night."

→✳THE✛RAVEN✳←

By Edgar Allan Poe.

ONCE upon a midnight dreary, while I pondered,
    weak and weary,
Over many a quaint and curious volume of
    forgotten lore,—
While I nodded, nearly napping, suddenly there
    came a tapping,
As of some one gently rapping, rapping at my chamber-door,
" 'Tis some visitor," I mutter'd, " tapping at my chamber-
    door—
        Only this, and nothing more."

Ah, distinctly I remember, it was in the bleak December,
And each separate dying ember wrought its ghost upon the
    floor.
Eagerly I wished the morrow; vainly I had sought to borrow
From my books surcease of sorrow—sorrow for the lost
    Lenore,—
For the rare and radiant maiden whom the angels name
    Lenore,—
        Nameless here forevermore.

And the silken, sad, uncertain rustling of each purple curtain,
Thrilled me,—filled me with fantastic terrors never felt
    before;

So that now, to still the beating of my heart, I stood repeating,
" 'Tis some visitor entreating entrance at my chamber-door,—
Some late visitor entreating entrance at my chamber-door;
       That it is, and nothing more."

Presently my soul grew stronger: hesitating then no longer,
" Sir," said I, " or Madam, truly your forgiveness I implore;
But the fact is, I was napping, and so gently you came rapping,
And so faintly you came tapping, tapping at my chamber-
       door,
That I scarce was sure I heard you"—here I opened wide the
       door:
       Darkness there, and nothing more.

Deep into that darkness peering, long I stood there, wonder-
       ing, fearing,
Doubting, dreaming dreams no mortals ever dared to dream
       before;
But the silence was unbroken, and the stillness gave no
       token,
And the only word there spoken was the whispered word,
       " Lenore ! "
This *I* whispered, and an echo murmured back the word,
       " LENORE ! "
       Merely this, and nothing more.

Back into the chamber turning, all my soul within me
       burning,
Soon again I heard a tapping, something louder than before.
" Surely," said I, " surely that is something at my window-
       lattice;
Let me see then what thereat is and this mystery explore,—
Let my heart be still a moment, and this mystery explore;—
       'Tis the wind, and nothing more."

Open here I flung the shutter, when, with many a flirt and
flutter,
In there stepped a stately raven of the saintly days of yore.
Not the least obeisance made he; not a minute stopped or
stayed he;
But, with mien of lord or lady, perched above my chamber-
door,—
Perched upon a bust of Pallas, just above my chamber-door—
Perched, and sat, and nothing more.

Then this ebony bird beguiling my sad fancy into smiling,
By the grave and stern decorum of the countenance it wore,
"Though thy crest be shorn and shaven, thou," I said, "art
sure no raven;
Ghastly, grim, and ancient raven, wandering from the nightly
shore,
Tell me what thy lordly name is on the night's Plutonian
shore ?"
Quoth the raven, "Nevermore!"

Much I marveled this ungainly fowl to hear discourse so
plainly,
Though its answer little meaning, little relevancy bore;
For we cannot help agreeing that no living human being
Ever yet was blessed with seeing bird above his chamber-
door,
Bird or beast upon the sculptured bust above his chamber-
door
With such name as "Nevermore!"

But the raven, sitting lonely on the placid bust, spoke only
That one word, as if his soul in that one word he did out-
pour,

Nothing further then he uttered; not a feather then he
    fluttered—
Till I scarcely more than muttered, " Other friends have
    flown before,
On the morrow *he* will leave me, as my hopes have flown
    before."
            Then the bird said, " Nevermore ! "

Startled at the stillness, broken by reply so aptly spoken,
" Doubtless," said I, " what it utters is its only stock and
    store,
Caught from some unhappy master, whom unmerciful disaster
Follow'd fast and follow'd faster, till his songs one burden
    bore,
Till the dirges of his hope that melancholy burden bore,
            Of—' Never—nevermore ! ' "

But the raven still beguiling all my sad soul into smiling,
Straight I wheeled a cushioned seat in front of bird and bust
    and door,
Then, upon the velvet sinking, I betook myself to linking
Fancy unto fancy, thinking what this ominous bird of yore—
What this grim, ungainly, ghastly, gaunt, and ominous bird
    of yore
            Meant in croaking " Nevermore ! "

This I sat engaged in guessing, but no syllable expressing
To the fowl whose fiery eyes now burn'd into my bosom's
    core;
This and more I sat divining, with my head at ease reclining
On the cushion's velvet lining that the lamp-light gloated
    o'er,
But whose velvet violet lining with the lamp-light gloating
    o'er
            She shall press—ah ! nevermore !

Then methought the air grew denser, perfumed from an
    unseen censer
Swung by seraphim, whose foot-falls tinkled on the tufted
    floor.
" Wretch," I cried, " thy God hath lent thee—by these angels
    he hath sent thee
Respite—respite and nepenthe from thy memories of Lenore!
Quaff, oh, quaff this kind nepenthe, and forget this lost
    Lenore ! "
            Quoth the raven, " Nevermore ! "

" Prophet ! " said I, " thing of evil!—prophet still, if bird
    or devil !
Whether tempter sent, or whether tempest tossed thee here
    ashore,
Desolate, yet all undaunted, on this desert land enchanted—
On this home by horror haunted—tell me truly, I implore,—
Is there—*is* there balm in Gilead ? — tell me—tell me, I im-
    plore ! "
Quoth the raven, " Nevermore ! "

" Prophet! " said I, " thing of evil!—prophet still, if bird
    or devil !
By that heaven that bends above us, by that God we both
    adore,
Tell this soul, with sorrow laden, if, within the distant
    Aidenn,
It shall clasp a sainted maiden, whom the angels name
    Lenore;
Clasp a rare and radiant maiden, whom the angels name
    Lenore ! "
            Quoth the raven, " Nevermore ! "

"Be that word our sign of parting, bird or fiend!" I
    shrieked, upstarting,—
"Get thee back into the tempest and the night's Plutonian
    shore!
Leave no black plume as a token of that lie thy soul hath
    spoken!
Leave my loneliness unbroken!—quit the bust above my
    door!
Take thy beak from out my heart, and take thy form from
    off my door!"
            Quoth the raven, "Nevermore!"

And the raven, never flitting, still is sitting, still is sitting
On the pallid bust of Pallas, just above my chamber-door;
And his eyes have all the seeming of a demon's that is
    dreaming,
And the lamp-light o'er him streaming throws his shadow
    on the floor;
And my soul from out that shadow that lies floating on the
    floor
            Shall be lifted—NEVERMORE!

MY PRETTY, BUDDING, BREATHING FLOWER

By WINTHROP MACKWORTH PRAED.

MY pretty, budding, breathing flower,
    Methinks, if I to-morrow
Could manage, just for half an hour,
    Sir Joshua's brush to borrow,
I might immortalize a few
    Of all the myriad graces
Which Time, while yet they all are new,
    With newer still replaces.

I'd paint, my child, your deep blue eyes,
    The quick and earnest flashes;
I'd paint the fringe that round them lies,
    The fringe of long dark lashes.
I'd draw with most fastidious care,
    One eyebrow, then the other;
And that fair forehead, broad and fair,—
    The forehead of your mother.

I'd oft retouch the dimpled cheek
    Where health in sunshine dances;
And oft the pouting lips, where speak
    A thousand voiceless fancies;
And the soft neck would keep me long,
    The neck, more smooth and snowy
Than ever yet in schoolboy's song
    Had Caroline and Chloe.

Nor less on those twin rounded arms
    My new-found skill would linger;
Nor less upon the rosy charms
    Of every tiny finger;
Nor slight the small feet, little one,
    So prematurely clever
That, though they neither walk nor run,
    I think they'd jump for ever.

But then your odd, endearing ways,—
    What study e'er could catch them?
Your aimless gestures, aimless plays—
    What canvas e'er could match them?
Your lively leap of merriment,
    Your murmur of petition,
Your serious silence of content,
    Your laugh of recognition.

Here were a puzzling toil, indeed,
    For Art's most fine creations!—
Grow on, sweet baby; we will need,
    To notice your transformations,

No picture of your form or face,
  Your waking or your sleeping,
But that which Love shall daily trace,
  And trust to Memory's keeping.

Hereafter, when revolving years
  Have made you tall and twenty,
And brought you blended hopes and fears,
  And sighs and slaves in plenty,
May those who watch our little saint
  Among her tasks and duties,
Feel all her virtues hard to paint,
  As we now deem her beauties.

THE ÷ WATER ÷ THAT ÷ HAS ÷ PASSED.

LISTEN to the water-mill,
  Through the live-long day,
How the clanking of the wheels
  Wears the hours away!
Languidly the autumn wind
  Stirs the greenwood leaves;
From the fields the reapers sing,
  Binding up the sheaves,
And a proverb haunts my mind,
  As a spell is cast:
"The mill will never grind
  With the water that has passed."

Take the lesson to thyself,
  Living heart and true;
Golden years are fleeting by,
  Youth is passing too;
Learn to make the most of life,
  Lose no happy day;
Time will never bring thee back
  Chances swept away.
Leave no tender word unsaid;
  Love while life shall last—
"The mill will never grind
  With the water that has passed."

Work while yet the daylight shines,
    Man of strength and will;
Never does the streamlet glide
    Useless by the mill.
Wait not until to-morrow's sun
    Beams upon the way;
All that thou canst call thy own
    Lies in thy to-day.
Power, intellect, and health,
    May not, cannot last;
" The mill will never grind
    With the water that has passed."

Oh, the wasted hours of life
    That have drifted by ;
Oh, the good we might have done,
    Lost without a sigh ;
Love that we might once have saved
    By a single word ;
Thoughts conceived, but never penned,
    Perishing unheard.
Take the proverb to thine heart,
    Take ! oh, hold it fast !—
" The mill will never grind
    With the water that has passed."

POSSESSION.

BY BAYARD TAYLOR.

I.

T was our wedding day
A month ago, dear heart, I hear you say.
If months, or years, or ages since have passed,
I know not: I have ceased to question Time.
I only know that once there pealed a chime
Of joyous bells, and then I held you fast,
And all stood back, and none my right denied,
And forth we walked: the world was free and wide
Before us. Since that day
I count my life: the Past is washed away.

II.

It was no dream, that vow:
It was the voice that woke me from a dream,—
A happy dream, I think; but I am waking now,
And drink the splendor of a sun supreme
That turns the mist of former tears to gold.
Within these arms I hold
The fleeting promise, chased so long in vain:
Ah, weary bird ! thou wilt not fly again:
Thy wings are clipped, thou canst no more depart,—
Thy nest is builded in my heart.

→❖WINTER.❖←

FROM "THE WINTER MORNING WALK."

BY WILLIAM COWPER.

'Tis morning; and the sun, with ruddy orb
Ascending, fires the horizon; while the clouds,
That crowd away before the driving wind,
More ardent as the disk emerges more,
Resemble most some city in a blaze,
Seen through the leafless wood. His slanting ray
Slides ineffectual down the snowy vale,
And, tingeing all with his own rosy hue,
From every herb and every spiry blade
Stretches a length of shadow o'er the field.
Mine, spindling into longitude immense,
In spite of gravity, and sage remark
That I myself am but a fleeting shade,
Provokes me to a smile. With eye askance
I view the muscular proportioned limb
Transformed to a lean shank. The shapeless pair,
As they designed to mock me, at my side
Take step for step; and, as I near approach
The cottage, walk along the plastered wall,
Preposterous sight! the legs without the man.

The verdure of the plain lies buried deep
Beneath the dazzling deluge; and the bents,
And coarser grass, upspearing o'er the rest,
Of late unsightly and unseen, now shine
Conspicuous, and in bright apparel clad,
And, fledged with icy feathers, nod superb.
The cattle mourn in corners, where the fence
Screens them, and seem half petrified to sleep
In unrecumbent sadness.   There they wait
Their wonted fodder; not, like hungry man,
Fretful if unsupplied; but silent, meek,
And, patient of the slow-paced swain's delay.
He from the stack carves out the accustomed load,
Deep plunging, and again deep plunging oft,
His broad keen knife into the solid mass:
Smooth as a wall the upright remnant stands,
With such undeviating and even force
He severs it away: no needless care
Lest storms should overset the leaning pile
Deciduous, or its own unbalanced weight.
Forth goes the woodman, leaving unconcerned
The cheerful haunts of man, to wield the axe
And drive the wedge in yonder forest drear,
From morn to eve his solitary task.
Shaggy and lean and shrewd with pointed ears,
And tail cropped short, half lurcher and half cur,
His dog attends him.   Close behind his heel
Now creeps he slow; and now, with many a frisk
Wide-scampering, snatches up the drifted snow
With ivory teeth, or ploughs it with his snout;
Then shakes his powdered coat, and barks for joy.

Now from the roost, or from the neighboring pile,

.   .   .   " There they wait their wonted fodder."

Where, diligent to catch the first faint gleam
Of smiling day, they gossiped side by side,
Come trooping at the housewife's well-known call
The feathered tribes domestic. Half on wing,
And half on foot, they brush the fleecy flood,
Conscious and fearful of too deep a plunge.
The sparrows peep, and quit the sheltering eaves
To seize the fair occasion. Well they eye
The scattered grain, and thievishly resolved
To escape the impending famine, often scared
As oft to return, a pert voracious kind.
Clean riddance quickly made, one only care
Remains to each, the search of sunny nook,
Or shed impervious to the blast. Resigned
To sad necessity, the cock foregoes
His wonted strut, and, wading at their head
With well-considered steps, seems to resent
His altered gait and stateliness retrenched.
How find the myriads, that in summer cheer
The hills and valleys with their ceaseless songs,
Due sustenance, or where subsist they now?
Earth yields them naught; the imprisoned worm is safe
Beneath the frozen clod; all seeds of herbs
Lie covered close; and berry-bearing thorns,
That feed the thrush (whatever some suppose),
Afford the smaller minstrels no supply.
The long protracted rigor of the year
Thins all their numerous flocks. In chinks and holes
Ten thousand seek an unmolested end,
An instinct prompts; self-buried ere they die.

➤✳KISS✦ME✦SOFTLY.✳◄

Da me basia.—CATULLUS.

BY JOHN GODFREY SAXE.

I.

KISS me softly and speak to me low,—
　　Malice has ever a vigilant ear,
　　What if Malice were lurking near?
　　　　Kiss me, dear!
Kiss me softly and speak to me low.

II.

Kiss me softly and speak to me low,—
　　Envy too has a watchful ear:
　　What if Envy should chance to hear?
　　　　Kiss me, dear!
Kiss me softly and speak to me low.

III.

Kiss me softly and speak to me low;
　　Trust me, darling, the time is near
　　When lovers may love with never a fear,—
　　　　Kiss me, dear!
Kiss me softly and speak to me low.

Around my ivied porch shall spring
Each fragrant flower that drinks the dew;
And Lucy, at her wheel, shall sing
In russet gown and apron blue.

The village-church among the trees,
Where first our marriage-vows were given,
With merry peals shall swell the breeze
And point with taper spire to heaven.

SHE IS NOT FAIR.

BY HARTLEY COLERIDGE.

SHE is not fair to outward view,
   As many maidens be;
Her loveliness I never knew
   Until she smiled on me:
O, then I saw her eye was bright,—
A well of love, a spring of light.

But now her looks are coy and cold;
   To mine they ne'er reply;
And yet I cease not to behold,
   The love-light in her eye:
Her very frowns are better far
Than smiles of other maidens are!

➤❈THE❈LITTLE❈MILLINER.❈◄

BY ROBERT BUCHANAN.

Y girl hath violet eyes and yellow hair,
A soft hand, like a lady's, small and fair,
A sweet face pouting in a white straw
    bonnet,
A tiny foot, and little boot upon it;
And all her finery to charm beholders
Is the gray shawl drawn tight around her
    shoulders,
The plain stuff-gown and collar white as
    snow,
And sweet red petticoat that peeps below.
But gladly in the busy town goes she,
Summer and winter, fearing nobodie;
She pats the pavement with her fairy feet,
With fearless eyes she charms the crowded street;
And in her pockets lie, in lieu of gold,
A lucky sixpence and a thimble old.

We lodged in the same house a year ago:
She on the topmost floor, I just below,—
She, a poor milliner, content and wise,
I, a poor city clerk, with hopes to rise;

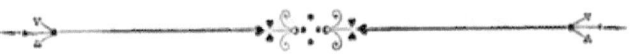

And, long ere we were friends, I learnt to love
The little angel on the floor above.
For, every morn, ere from my bed I stirred,
Her chamber door would open, and I heard,—
And listened, blushing to, her coming down,
And palpitated with her rustling gown,
And tingled while her foot went downward slow,
Creaked like a cricket, passed, and died below;
Then peeping from the window, pleased and sly,
I saw the pretty shining face go by,
Healthy and rosy, fresh from slumber sweet,—
A sunbeam in the quiet morning street.

And every night, when in from work she tript,
Red to the ears I from my chamber slipt,
That I might hear upon the narrow stair
Her low "Good evening," as she passed me there.
And when her door was closed, below sat I,
And hearkened stilly as she stirred on high,—
Watched the red firelight shadows in the room,
Fashioned her face before me in the gloom,
And heard her close the window, lock the door,
Moving about more lightly than before,
And thought, " She is undressing now ! " and O,
My cheeks were hot, my heart was in a glow !
And I made pictures of her,—standing bright
Before the looking-glass in bed-gown white,
Unbinding in a knot her yellow hair,
Then kneeling timidly to say a prayer;
Till, last, the floor creaked softly overhead,
'Neath bare feet tripping to the little bed,—
And all was hushed.   Yet still I hearkened on,
Till the faint sounds about the streets were gone;

And saw her slumbering with lips apart,
One little hand upon her little heart,
The other pillowing a face that smiled
In slumber like the slumber of a child,
The bright hair shining round the small white ear,
The soft breath stealing visible and clear,
And mixing with the moon's, whose frosty gleam
Made round her rest a vaporous light of dream.

How free she wandered in the wicked place,
Protected only by her gentle face !
She saw bad things—how could she choose but see ?
She heard of wantonness and misery;
The city closed around her night and day,
But lightly, happily, she went her way.
Nothing of evil that she saw or heard
Could touch a heart so innocently stirred,—
By simple hopes that cheered it through the storm,
And little flutterings that kept it warm.
No power had she to reason out her needs,
To give the whence and wherefore of her deeds;
But she was good and pure amid the strife,
By virtue of the joy that was her life.
Here, where a thousand spirits daily fall,
Where heart and soul and senses turn to gall,
She floated, pure as innocence could be,
Like a small sea-bird on a stormy sea,
Which breasts the billows, wafted to and fro,
Fearless, uninjured, while the strong winds blow,
While the clouds gather, and the waters roar,
And mighty ships are broken on the shore.

'T was when the spring was coming, when the snow
Had melted, and fresh winds began to blow,
And girls were selling violets in the town,
That suddenly a fever struck me down.
The world was changed, the sense of life was pained,
And nothing but a shadow-land remained;
Death came in a dark mist and looked at me,
I felt his breathing, though I could not see,
But heavily I lay and did not stir,
And had strange images and dreams of her.
Then came a vacancy: with feeble breath
I shivered under the cold touch of Death,
And swooned among strange visions of the dead,
When a voice called from heaven, and he fled;
And suddenly I wakened, as it seemed
From a deep sleep wherein I had not dreamed.

And it was night, and I could see and hear,
And I was in the room I held so dear,
And unaware, stretched out upon my bed,
I hearkened for a footstep overhead.

But all was hushed.   I looked around the room,
And slowly made out shapes amid the gloom.
The wall was reddened by a rosy light,
A faint fire flickered, and I knew 't was night,
Because below there was a sound of feet
Dying away along the quiet street,—
When, turning my pale face and sighing low,
I saw a vision in the quiet glow:
A little figure, in a cotton gown,
Looking upon the fire and stooping down,

Her side to me, her face illumined, she eyed
Two chestnuts burning slowly, side by side,—
Her lips apart, her clear eyes strained to see,
Her little hands clasped tight around her knee,
The firelight gleaming on her golden head,
And tinting her white neck to rosy red,
Her features bright, and beautiful, and pure,
With childish fear and yearning half demure.

O sweet, sweet dream ! I thought, and strained mine eyes,
Fearing to break the spell with words and sighs.
Softly she stooped, her dear face sweetly fair,
And sweeter since a light like love was there,
Brightening, watching, more and more elate,
As the nuts glowed together in the grate,
Crackling with little jets of fiery light,
Till side by side they turned to ashes white,—
Then up she leapt, her face cast off its fear
For rapture that itself was radiance clear,
And would have clapped her little hands in glee,
But, pausing, bit her lips and peeped at me,
And met the face that yearned on her so whitely,
And gave a cry and trembled, blushing brightly,
While, raised on elbow, as she turned to flee,
" Polly!" I cried,—and grew as red as she !

It was no dream ! for soon my thoughts were clear,
And she could tell me all, and I could hear:
How in my sickness friendless I had lain,
How the hard people pitied not my pain;
How, in spite of what bad people said,
She left her labors, stopped beside my bed,

And nursed me, thinking sadly I would die;
How, in the end, the danger passed me by;
How she had sought to steal away before
The sickness passed, and I was strong once more.
By fits she told the story in mine ear,
And troubled all the telling with a fear
Lest by my cold man's heart she should be chid,
Lest I should think her bold in what she did;
But, lying on my bed, I dared to say,
How I had watched and loved her many a day,
How dear she was to me, and dearer still
For that strange kindness done while I was ill,
And how I could but think that Heaven above
Had done it all to bind our lives in love.
And Polly cried, turning her face away,
And seemed afraid, and answered "yea" nor "nay";
Then stealing close, with little pants and sighs,
Looked on my pale thin face and earnest eyes,
And seemed in act to fling her arms about
My neck, then, blushing, paused, in flattering doubt,
Last, sprang upon my heart, sighing and sobbing,—
That I might feel how gladly hers was throbbing!

Ah! ne'er shall I forget until I die
How happily the dreamy days went by,
While I grew well, and lay with soft heart-beats,
Heark'ning the pleasant murmur from the streets,
And Polly·by me like a sunny beam,
And life all changed, and love a drowsy dream!
'T was happiness enough to lie and see
The little golden head bent droopingly
Over its sewing, while the still time flew,
And my fond eyes were dim with happy dew!

And then, when I was nearly well and strong,
And she went back to labor all day long,
How sweet to lie alone with half-shut eyes,
And hear the distant murmurs and the cries,
And think how pure she was from pain and sin,—
And how the summer days were coming in!
Then, as the sunset faded from the room,
To listen for her footstep in the gloom,
To pant as it came stealing up the stair,
To feel my whole life brighten unaware
When the soft tap came to the door, and when
The door was opened for her smile again!
Best, the long evenings!—when, till late at night,
She sat beside me in the quiet light,
And happy things were said and kisses won,
And serious gladness found its vent in fun.
Sometimes I would draw close her shining head,
And pour her bright hair out upon the bed,
And she would laugh, and blush, and try to scold,
While "Here," I cried, "I count my wealth in gold!"

Once, like a little sinner for transgression,
She blushed upon my breast, and made confession:
How, when that night I woke and looked around,
I found her busy with a charm profound,—
One chestnut was herself, my girl confessed,
The other was the person she loved best,
And if they burned together side by side,
He loved her, and she would become his bride;
And burn indeed they did, to her delight,—
And had the pretty charm not proven right?
Thus much, and more, with timorous joy, she said,
While her confessor, too, grew rosy red,—

And close together pressed two blissful faces,
As I absolved the sinner, with embraces.

    And here is winter come again, winds blow,
The houses and the streets are white with snow;
And in the long and pleasant eventide,
Why, what is Polly making at my side?
What but a silk gown, beautiful and grand,
We bought together lately in the Strand!
What but a dress to go to church in soon,
And wear right queenly 'neath a honey-moon!
And who shall match her with her new straw bonnet,
Her tiny foot and little boot upon it,
Embroidered petticoat and silk gown new,
And shawl she wears as few fine ladies do?
And she will keep, to charm away all ill,
The lucky sixpence in her pocket still;
And we will turn, come fair or cloudy weather,
To ashes, like the chestnuts, close together!

➤✲SMALL ✦ BEGINNINGS.✲◄

BY CHARLES MACKAY.

A TRAVELER through a dusty road strewed
    acorns on the lea;
And one took root and sprouted up, and
    grew into a tree.
Love sought its shade, at evening time, to
    breathe its early vows;
And age was pleased, in heats of noon, to
    bask beneath its boughs;
The dormouse loved its dangling twigs, the
    birds sweet music bore;
It stood a glory in its place, a blessing
    evermore.

A little spring had lost its way amid the grass and fern,
A passing stranger scooped a well, where weary men might
    turn;
He walled it in, and hung with care a ladle at the brink;
He thought not of the deed he did, but judged that toil
    might drink.
He passed again, and lo ! the well, by summers never dried,
Had cooled ten thousand parching tongues, and saved a
    life beside.

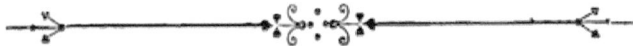

A dreamer dropped a random thought; 't was old, and yet
    't was new;
A simple fancy of the brain, but strong in being true.
It shone upon a genial mind, and lo! its light became
A lamp of life, a beacon ray, a monitory flame.
The thought was small; its issue great; a watch-fire on
    the hill;
It sheds its radiance far adown, and. cheers the valley
    still !

A nameless man amid a crowd that thronged the daily
    mart,
Let fall a word of Hope and Love, unstudied, from the
    heart;
A whisper on the tumult thrown,—a transitory breath,—
It raised a brother from the dust; it saved a soul from
    death.
O germ ! O fount ! O word of love ! O thought at random
    cast !
Ye were but little at the first, but mighty at the last.

⋆✷MY⋆MOTHER.✷⋆

That was a thrilling scene in the old chivalric time—the wine circling round the board, and the banquet-hall ringing with sentiment and song—when the lady of each knightly heart having been pledged by name, St. Leon arose in his turn, and, lifting the sparkling cup on high, said: "I drink to one

HOSE image never may depart,
Deep graven on this grateful heart,
   Till memory is dead;

To one whose love for me shall last
When lighter passions long have passed,
   So holy 'tis, and true;

To one whose love hath longer dwelt,
More deeply fixed, more keenly felt,
   Than any pledge to you."

Each guest upstarted at the word,
And laid his hand upon his sword,
   With fury-flashing eyes;

And Stanley said, "We crave the name,
Proud knight, of this most peerless dame;
   Whose love you count so high."

St. Leon paused, as if he would
Not breathe her name in careless mood
   Thus lightly to another—

Then bent his noble head, as though
To give that word the reverence due,
   And gently said, "My mother."

➤✳THE✥VALE✥OF✥CASHMERE.✳←

FROM "THE LIGHT OF THE HAREM."

BY THOMAS MOORE.

HO has not heard of the Vale of Cashmere,
  With its roses the brightest that earth ever
    gave,
  Its temples, and grottos, and fountains as clear
    As the love-lighted eyes that hang over
      their wave?

O, to see it at sunset,—when warm o'er the lake
  Its splendor at parting a summer eve throws,
Like a bride, full of blushes, when lingering to take
  A last look of her mirror at night ere she goes!—
When the shrines through the foliage are gleaming half shown,
And each hallows the hour by some rites of its own.
Here the music of prayer from a minaret swells,
  Here the Magian his urn full of perfume is swinging,
And here, at the altar, a zone of sweet bells
  Round the waist of some fair Indian dancer is ringing.
Or to see it by moonlight,—when mellowly shines
The light o'er its palaces, gardens, and shrines;
When the waterfalls gleam like a quick fall of stars,
And the nightingale's hymn from the Isle of Chenars
Is broken by laughs and light echoes of feet
From the cool shining walks where the young people meet.

"Its temples, and grottos, and fountains as clear
As the love-lighted eyes that hang over their wave."

Or at morn, when the magic of daylight awakes
A new wonder each minute as slowly it breaks,
Hills, cupolas, fountains, called forth every one
Out of darkness, as they were just born of the sun.
When the spirit of fragrance is up with the day,
From his harem of night-flowers stealing away;
And the wind, full of wantonness, woos, like a lover
The young aspen-trees till they tremble all over.
When the east is as warm as the light of first hopes,
    And day, with its banner of radiance unfurled,
Shines in through the mountainous portal that opes,
    Sublime, from that valley of bliss to the world !

➤✳MOLLY✚CAREW✳◄

TO THE HARD-HEARTED MOLLY CAREW—THE LAMENT
OF HER IRISH LOVER.

BY FATHER PROUT.

CH hone!
Oh! what will I do?
Sure my love is all crost,
Like a bud in the frost . . .
And there's no use at all
In my going to bed;
For 'tis dhrames, and not sleep,
That comes into my head . . .
And 'tis all about you,
My sweet Molly Carew,
And indeed 'tis a sin
And a shame.
You're complater than nature
In every feature;
The snow can't compare
To your forehead so fair;
And I rather would spy
Just one blink of your eye
Than the purtiest star
That shines out of the sky;

Tho'—by this and by that !
For the matter o' that—
You're more distant by far
Than that same.
        Och hone, wierasthrew !
I am alone
In this world without you !

Och hone !
        But why should I speak
Of your forehead and eyes,
When your nose it defies
Paddy Blake the schoolmaster
        To put it in rhyme ? —
Though there's one BURKE,
He says,
Who would call it *Snub*lime . . .
        And then for your cheek,
Throth, 'twould take him a week
Its beauties to tell
As he'd rather:—
        Then your lips, O machree !
In their beautiful glow
They a pattern might be
For the cherries to grow.
'Twas an apple that tempted
Our mother, we know;
For apples were scarce
I suppose long ago:
But at this time o' day
'Pon my conscience I'll say,
Such cherries might tempt .
A man's father !

Och hone, wierasthrew !
I'm alone
In this world without you !

Och hone !
      By the man in the moon !
You tease me all ways
That a woman can plaze;
For you dance twice as high
With that thief Pat Macghee
As when you take share
Of a jig, dear, with me;
      Though the piper I bate,
For fear the ould chate
Wouldn't play you your
Favorite tune.
      And when you're at Mass
My devotion you crass,
For 'tis thinking of you
I am, Molly Carew;
While you wear on purpose
A bonnet so deep,
That I can't at your sweet
Pretty face get a peep.
Oh ! lave off that bonnet,
Or else I'll lave on it
The loss of my wandering
Sowl !
      Och hone ! like an owl,
Day is night,
Dear, to me without you !

Och hone !
      Don't provoke me to do it;

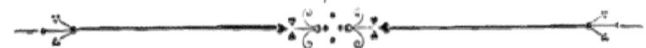

For there's girls by the score
That loves me, and more.

    And you'd look very queer,
If some morning you'd meet
My wedding all marching
In pride down the street.

    Troth you'd open your eyes,
And you'd die of surprise
To think 'twasn't you
Was come to it.

    And faith ! Kitty Naile
And her cow, I go bail,
Would jump if I'd say,
" Kitty Naile, name the day."
And though you're fair and fresh
As the blossoms of May,
And she's short and dark
Like a cowld winter's day,
Yet, if *you* don't repent
Before Easter—when Lent
Is over—I'll marry
For spite.

    Och hone ! and when I
Die for you,
'Tis my ghost that you'll see every night.

THE ORIGIN OF THE OPAL.

ANONYMOUS.

A DEW-DROP came, with a spark of flame
    He had caught from the sun's last ray,
To a violet's breast, where he lay at rest
    Till the hours brought back the day.

The rose looked down, with a blush and
    frown;
    But she smiled all at once, to view
Her own bright form, with its coloring warm,
    Reflected back by the dew.

Then the stranger took a stolen look
    At the sky, so soft and blue;
And a leaflet green, with its silver sheen,
    Was seen by the idler too.

A cold north-wind, as he thus reclined,
    Of a sudden raged around;
And a maiden fair, who was walking there,
    Next morning, an *opal* found.

✳MAN✛WAS✛MADE✛TO✛MOURN.✳

BY ROBERT BURNS.

WHEN chill November's surly blast,
  Made fields and forests bare,
One evening, as I wander'd forth
  Along the banks of Ayr,
I spied a man, whose aged step
  Seem'd weary, worn with care;
His face was furrow'd o'er with years,
  And hoary was his hair.

Young stranger, whither wanderest thou?
  (Began the reverend sage;)
Dost thirst of wealth thy step constrain,
  Or youthful pleasures rage?
Or haply, prest with cares and woes,
  Too soon thou hast began,
To wander forth, with me, to mourn
  The miseries of man!

The sun that overhangs yon moors,
  Out-spreading far and wide,
Where hundreds labor to support
  A haughty lordling's pride;

I've seen yon weary winter-sun
    Twice forty times return;
And every time has added proofs
    That man was made to mourn.

O man ! while in thy early years,
    How prodigal of time !
Mis-spending all thy precious hours
    Thy glorious youthful prime !
Alternate follies take the sway;
    Licentious passions burn;
Which tenfold force give Nature's law,
    That man was made to mourn.

Look not alone on youthful prime,
    Or manhood's active might:
Man then is useful to his kind,
    Supported is his right.
But see him on the edge of life,
    With cares and sorrows worn,
Then age and want, oh ! ill-matched pair,
    Show man was made to mourn.

A few seem favorites of fate,
    In pleasure's lap carest;
Yet, think not all the rich and great
    Are likewise truly blest.
But, oh ! what crowds, in every land,
    Are wretched and forlorn;
Through weary life this lesson learn,
    That man was made to mourn.

Many and sharp the numerous ills
 Inwoven with our frame !
More pointed still we make ourselves,
 Regret, remorse, and shame !
And man, whose heaven-erected face
 The smiles of love adorn,
Man's inhumanity to man
 Makes countless thousands mourn !

See yonder poor, o'erlabor'd wight,
 So abject, mean, and vile,
Who begs a brother of the earth,
 To give him leave to toil:
And see his lordly fellow-worm
 The poor petition spurn,
Unmindful, though a weeping wife
 And helpless offspring mourn.

If I'm design'd yon lordling's slave—
 By Nature's law design'd,
Why was an independent wish
 E'er planted in my mind ?
If not, why am I subject to
 His cruelty or scorn ?
Or why has man the will and power
 To make his fellow mourn ?

Yet, let not this too much, my son,
 Disturb thy youthful breast:
This partial view of human-kind
 Is surely not the last !

The poor, oppressed, honest man,
    Had never, sure, been born,
Had there not been some recompense
    To comfort those that mourn!

O Death! the poor man's dearest friend,
    The kindest and the best!
Welcome the hour my aged limbs
    Are laid with thee at rest!
The great, the wealthy, fear thy blow,
    From pomp and pleasure torn;
But, oh! a blest relief to those
    That weary-laden mourn!

THE CHILDREN.

BY CHARLES DICKENS.

HEN the lessons and tasks are all ended,
　　And the school for the day is dismissed,
And the little ones gather around me,
　　To bid the good-night and be kissed;
Oh, the little white arms that encircle
　　My neck in a tender embrace !
Oh, the smiles that are halos of heaven,
　　Shedding sunshine of love on my face !

And when they are gone I sit dreaming
　　Of my childhood too lovely to last:
Of love that my heart will remember,
　　When it wakes to the pulse of the past,
Ere the world and its wickedness made me
　　A partner of sorrow and sin,
When the glory of God was about me,
　　And the glory of gladness within.

Oh, my heart grows weak as a woman's,
　　And the fountains of feeling will flow,
When I think of the paths, steep and stony,
　　Where the feet of the dear ones must go;

Of the mountains of sin hanging o'er them,
   Of the tempest of Fate blowing wild;
Oh ! there is nothing on earth half so holy,
   As the innocent heart of a child !

They are idols of hearts and of households,
   They are angels of God in disguise;
His sunlight still sleeps in their tresses,
   His glory still gleams in their eyes;
Oh ! those truants from home and from heaven,
   They have made me more manly and mild !
And I know how Jesus could liken
   The Kingdom of God to a child.

Seek not a life for the dear ones,
   All radiant as others have done,
But that life may have just enough shadow
   To temper the glare of the sun;
I would pray God to guard them from evil,
   But my prayer would bound back to myself.
Ah ! a seraph may pray for a sinner,
   But a sinner must pray for himself.

The twig is so easily bended,
   I have banished the rule and the rod;
I have taught them the goodness of knowledge,
   They have taught me the goodness of God;
My heart is a dungeon of darkness,
   Where I shut them from breaking a rule:
My frown is sufficient correction;
   My love is the law of the school.

I shall leave the old house in the autumn,
　　To traverse its threshold no more;
Ah! how I shall sigh for the dear ones,
　　That meet me each morn at the door!
I shall miss the "good-nights" and the kisses,
　　And the gush of their innocent glee,
The group on the green and the flowers
　　That are brought every morning to me.

I shall miss them at morn and at eve,
　　Their song in the school and the street:
I shall miss the low hum of their voices
　　And the tramp of their delicate feet.
When the lessons and tasks are all ended,
　　And death says, " The school is dismissed ! "
May the little ones gather around me,
　　To bid me good-night and be kissed.

HUNTING SONG.

BY SIR WALTER SCOTT.

WAKEN, lords and ladies gay !
On the mountain dawns the day;
All the jolly chase is here,
With hawk, and horse, and hunting-spear;
Hounds are in their couples yelling,
Hawks are whistling, horns are knelling,
Merrily, merrily mingle they,—
" Waken, lords and ladies gay."

Waken, lords and ladies gay !
The mist has left the mountain gray,
Springlets in the dawn are streaming,
Diamonds on the brake are gleaming,
And foresters have busy been
To track the buck in thicket green;
Now we come to chant our lay.—
" Waken, lords and ladies gay."

Waken, lords and ladies gay !
To the greenwood haste away;
We can show you where he lies,
Fleet of foot, and tall of size;

" We can show you where he lies,
Fleet of foot, and tall of size."

We can show the marks he made
When 'gainst the oak his antlers frayed;
You shall see him brought to bay;
" Waken, lords and ladies gay."

Louder, louder chant the lay,
" Waken, lords and ladies gay ! "
Tell them youth, and mirth, and glee,
Run a course as well as we;
Time, stern huntsman ! who can baulk,
Stanch as hound and fleet as hawk;
Think of this, and rise with day,
Gentle lords and ladies gay !

THE GREENWOOD SHRIFT.

A SCENE IN WINDSOR FOREST, ENGLAND.

BY ROBERT SOUTHEY.

OUTSTRETCHED beneath the leafy shade
Of Windsor forest's deepest glade,
   A dying woman lay;
Three little children round her stood,
And there went up from the greenwood
   A woful wail that day.

"O mother!" was the mingled cry,
"O mother, mother! do not die,
   And leave us all alone."
"My blessed babes!" she tried to say,
But the faint accents died away
   In a low sobbing moan.

And then, life struggling hard with death,
And fast and strong she drew her breath,
   And up she raised her head;
And, peering through the deep wood maze
With a long, sharp, unearthly gaze,
   "Will she not come?" she said.

Just then the parting boughs between,
A little maid's light form was seen,
    All breathless with her speed;
And following close a man came on
(A portly man to look upon,)
    Who led a panting steed.

" Mother ! " the little maiden cried,
Or e'er she reached the woman's side,
    And kissed her clay-cold cheek,—
" I have not idled in the town,
But long went wandering up and down,
    The minister to seek.

" They told me here, they told me there,—
I think they mocked me everywhere;
    And when I found his home,
And begged him on my bended knee
To bring his book and come with me,
    Mother ! he would not come.

" I told him how you dying lay,
And could not go in peace away
    Without the minister:
I begged him, for dear Christ his sake,
But O, my heart was fit to break,—
    Mother ! he would not stir.

" So, though my tears were blinding me,
I ran back, fast as fast could be,
    To come again to you;
And here—close by—this squire I met,
Who asked, so mild, what made me fret;
    And when I told him true,—

"'I will go with you, child,' he said,
'God sends me to this dying bed,'—
    Mother, he's here, hard by."
While thus the little maiden spoke,
The man, his back against an oak,
    Looked on with glistening eye.

The bridle on his neck hung free,
With quivering flank and trembling knee,
    Pressed close his bonny bay;
A statelier man, a statelier steed,
Never on greensward paced, I rede,
    Than those stood there that day.

So, while the little maiden spoke,
The man, his back against an oak,
    Looked on with glistening eye
And folded arms, and in his look
Something that, like a sermon-book,
    Preached,—"All is vanity."

But when the dying woman's face
Turned toward him with a wishful gaze,
    He stepped to where she lay;
And, kneeling down, bent over her,
Saying, "I am a minister,
    My sister! let us pray."

And well, withouten book or stole,
(God's words were printed on his soul!)
    Into the dying ear
He breathed, as 'twere an angel's strain,
The things that unto life pertain,
    And death's dark shadows clear.

He spoke of sinners' lost estate,
In Christ renewed, regenerate,—
     Of God's most blest decree,
That not a single soul should die
Who turns repentant, with the cry
     " Be merciful to me."

He spoke of trouble, pain, and toil,
Endured but for a little while
     In patience, faith, and love,—
Sure, in God's own good time, to be
Exchanged for an eternity
     Of happiness above.

Then as the spirit ebbed away,
He raised his hands and eyes to pray
     That peaceful it might pass;
And then—the orphan's sobs alone
Were heard, and they knelt, every one
     Close round on the green grass.

Such was the sight their wandering eyes
Beheld, in heart-struck, mute surprise,
     Who reined their coursers back.
Just as they found the long astray,
Who, in the heat of chase that day,
     Had wandered from their track.

But each man reined his pawing steed,
And lighted down, as if agreed,
     In silence at his side,
And there, uncovered all, they stood,—
It was a wholesome sight and good
     That day for mortal pride.

For of the noblest of the land
Was that deep-hushed, bareheaded band;
    And central in the ring,
By that dead pauper on the ground,
Her ragged orphans clinging round,
    *Knelt their anointed king.**

*George III.

→*THE+AMERICAN+FLAG.*←

BY JOSEPH RODMAN DRAKE.

WHEN Freedom, from her mountain height,
    Unfurled her standard to the air,
She tore the azure robe of night,
    And set the stars of glory there!
She mingled with its gorgeous dyes
The milky baldric of the skies,
And striped its pure, celestial white
With streakings of the morning light,
Then, from his mansion in the sun,
She called her eagle-bearer down,
And gave into his mighty hand
The symbol of her chosen land!

Majestic monarch of the cloud!
    Who rear'st aloft thy regal form,
To hear the tempest-trumpings loud,
And see the lightning lances driven,
    When strive the warriors of the storm,

And rolls the thunder-drum of heaven,—
Child of the Sun ! to thee 't is given
    To guard the banner of the free,
To hover in the sulphur smoke,
To ward away the battle-stroke,
And bid its blendings shine afar,
Like rainbows on the cloud of war,
    The harbingers of victory !

Flag of the brave ! thy folds shall fly,
The sign of hope and triumph high !
When speaks the signal-trumpet tone,
And the long line comes gleaming on,
Ere yet the life-blood, warm and wet,
Has dimmed the glistening bayonet,
Each soldier's eye shall brighty turn
To where thy sky-born glories burn,
And, as his springing steps advance,
Catch war and vengeance from the glance.
And when the cannon-mouthings loud
Heave in wild wreaths the battle shroud,
And gory sabres rise and fall
Like shoots of flame on midnight's pall,
Then shall thy meteor glances glow,
    And cowering foes shall shrink beneath
Each gallant arm that strikes below
    That lovely messenger of death.

Flag of the seas ! on ocean wave
Thy stars shall glitter o'er the brave;
When death, careering on the gale,
Sweeps darkly round the bellied sail,

And frighted waves rush wildly back
Before the broadside's reeling rack,
Each dying wanderer of the sea
Shall look at once to heaven and thee,
And smile to see thy splendors fly
In triumph o'er his closing eye.

Flag of the free heart's hope and home,
    By angel hands to valor given,
Thy stars have lit the welkin dome,
    And all thy hues were born in heaven.
Forever float that standard sheet!
    Where breathes the foe but falls before us,
With Freedom's soil beneath our feet,
    And Freedom's banner streaming o'er us!

COLUMBIA.

BY TIMOTHY DWIGHT.

COLUMBIA, Columbia, to glory arise,
The queen of the world, and child of the skies!
Thy genius commands thee; with rapture behold,
While ages on ages thy splendors unfold.
Thy reign is the last and the noblest of time,
Most fruitful thy soil, most inviting thy clime;
Let the crimes of the east ne'er encrimson thy name,
Be freedom and science and virtue thy fame.

To conquest and slaughter let Europe aspire;
Whelm nations in blood, and wrap cities in fire;
Thy heroes the rights of mankind shall defend,
And triumph pursue them, and glory attend.
A world is thy realm; for a world be thy laws,
Enlarged as thine empire, and just as thy cause;
On Freedom's broad basis that empire shall rise,
Extend with the main, and dissolve with the skies.

Fair Science her gates to thy sons shall unbar,
And the east see thy morn hide the beams of her star,
New bards and new sages unrivalled shall soar
To fame unextinguished when time is no more.
To thee, the last refuge of virtue designed,
Shall fly from all nations the best of mankind;
Here grateful to heaven, with transport shall bring
Their incense, more fragrant than odors of spring.

Nor less shall thy fair ones to glory ascend,
And genius and beauty in harmony blend;
The graces of form shall awake pure desire,
And the charms of the soul ever cherish the fire; ,
Their sweetness unmingled, their manners refined,
And virtue's bright image, enstamped on the mind,
With peace and soft rapture shall teach life to glow,
And light up a smile on the aspect of woe.

Thy fleets to all regions thy power shall display,
The nations admire, and the ocean obey;
Each shore to thy glory its tribute unfold,
And the east and the south yield their spices and gold.
As the dayspring unbounded thy splendor shall flow,
And earth's little kingdoms before thee shall bow,
While the ensigns of union, in triumph unfurled,
Hush the tumult of war, and give peace to the world.

Thus, as down a lone valley, with 'cedars o'erspread,
From war's dread confusion, I pensively strayed,—
The gloom from the face of fair heaven retired;
The winds ceased to murmur, the thunders expired;
Perfumes, as of Eden, flowed sweetly along,
And a voice, as of angels, enchantingly sung:
" Columbia, Columbia, to glory arise,
The queen of the world, and the child of the skies."

→✳MY✛COUNTRY.✳←

BY JAMES MONTGOMERY.

THERE is a land, of every land the pride,
Beloved by Heaven o'er all the world beside,
Where brighter suns dispense serener light,
And milder moons imparadise the night;
A land of beauty, virtue, valor, truth,
Time-tutored age, and love-exalted youth:
The wandering mariner, whose eye explores
The wealthiest isles, the most enchanting shores,
Views not a realm so bountiful and fair,
Nor breathes the spirit of a purer air.
In every clime, the magnet of his soul,
Touched by remembrance, trembles to that pole;
For in this land of Heaven's peculiar race,
The heritage of nature's noblest grace,
There is a spot of earth supremely blest,
A dearer, sweeter spot than all the rest,
Where man, creation's tyrant, casts aside
His sword and sceptre, pageantry and pride,
While in his softened looks benignly blend
The sire, the son, the husband, brother, friend.
Here woman reigns; the mother, daughter, wife,
Strew with fresh flowers the narrow way of life:

In the clear heaven of her delightful eye,
An angel-guard of love and graces lie;
Around her knees domestic duties meet,
And fireside pleasures gambol at her feet.
" Where shall that land, that spot of earth be found ? "
Art thou a man ? — a patriot ? — look around;
O, thou shalt find, howe'er thy footsteps roam,
That land *thy* country, and that spot *thy* home !

Man, through all ages of revolving time,
Unchanging man, in every varying clime,
Deems his own land of every land the pride,
Beloved by Heaven o'er all the world beside;
His home the spot of earth supremely blest,
A dearer, sweeter spot than all the rest.

➤✳A✛COURT✛LADY.✳⬅

BY ELIZABETH BARRETT BROWNING.

I.

HER hair was tawny with gold, her eyes with
　　purple were dark,
Her cheeks' pale opal burnt with a red
　　and restless spark.

II.

Never was lady of Milan nobler in name
　　and in race;
Never was lady of Italy fairer to see in
　　the face.

III.

Never was lady on earth more true as woman and wife,
Larger in judgment and instinct, prouder in manners and life.

IV

She stood in the early morning, and said to her maidens,
　　"Bring
That silken robe made ready to wear at the court of the king.

V.

"Bring me the clasps of diamonds, lucid, clear of the mote,
Clasp me the large at the waist, and clasp me the small at the
　　throat.

VI.

"Diamonds to fasten the hair, and diamonds to fasten the
sleeves,
Laces to drop from their rays, like a powder of snow from
the eaves."

VII.

Gorgeous she entered the sunlight which gathered her up in
a flame,
While, straight in her open carriage, she to the hospital
came.

VIII.

In she went at the door, and gazing, from end to end,
"Many and low are the pallets, but each is the place of a
friend."

IX.

Up she passed through the wards, and stood at a young
man's bed:
Bloody the band on his brow, and livid the droop of his
head.

X.

"Art thou a Lombard, my brother? Happy are thou!" she
cried,
And smiled like Italy on him: he dreamed in her face and
died.

XI.

Pale with his passing soul, she went on still to a second:
He was a grave hard man, whose years by dungeons were
reckoned.

XII.

Wounds in his body were sore, wounds in his life were sorer.
"Art thou a Romagnole?" Her eyes drove lightnings
   before her.

XIII.

"Austrian and priest had joined to double and tighten the
   cord
Able to bind thee, O strong one,—free by the stroke of a
   sword.

XIV.

"Now be grave for the rest of us, using the life overcast
To ripen our wine of the present (too new) in glooms of the
   past."

XV.

Down she stepped to a pallet where lay a face like a girl's,
Young, and pathetic with dying,—a deep black hole in the
   curls.

XVI.

"Art thou from Tuscany, brother? and seest thou, dreaming
   in pain,
Thy mother stand in the piazza, searching the list of the
   slain?"

XVII.

Kind as a mother herself, she touched his cheeks with her
   hands:
"Blessed is she who has born thee, although she should
   weep as she stands."

XVIII.

On she passed to a Frenchman, his arm carried off by a ball:
Kneeling, . . "O more than my brother! how shall I thank
thee for all?

XIX.

" Each of the heroes around us has fought for his land and
line,
But *thou* hast fought for a stranger, in hate of a wrong not
thine.

XX.

" Happy are all free peoples, too strong to be dispossessed.
But blessed are those among nations who dare to be strong
for the rest!"

XXI.

Ever she passed on her way, and came to a couch where
pined
One with a face from Venetia, white with a hope out of
mind.

XXII.

Long she stood and gazed, and twice she tried at the name,
But two great crystal tears were all that faltered and came.

XXIII.

Only a tear for Venice? — she turned as in passion and loss,
And stooped to his forehead and kissed it, as if she were
kissing the cross.

XXIV.

Faint with that strain of heart, she moved on then to another,
Stern and strong in his death. "And dost thou suffer, my
brother?"

XXV.

Holding his hands in hers : — "Out of the Piedmont lion
Cometh the sweetness of freedom! sweetest to live or to
    die on."

XXVI.

Holding his cold rough hands,—"Well, O, well have ye done
In noble, noble Piedmont, who would not be noble alone."

XXVII.

Back he fell while she spoke. She rose to her feet with a
    spring—
"That was a Piedmontese! and this is the Court of the
    King."

NAPOLEON ÷ AND ÷ THE ÷ BRITISH ÷ SAILOR.

BY THOMAS CAMPBELL.

LOVE contemplating—apart
    From all his homicidal glory—
The traits that soften to our heart
    Napoleon's glory!

'T was when his banners at Boulogne
    Armed in our island every freeman,
His navy chanced to capture one
    Poor British seaman.

They suffered him—I know not how—
    Unprisoned on the shore to roam;
And aye was bent his longing brow
    On England's home.

His eye, methinks! pursued the flight
    Of birds to Britain half-way over;
With envy *they* could reach the white
    Dear cliffs of Dover.

A stormy midnight watch, he thought,
    Than this sojourn would have been dearer,
If but the storm his vessel brought
    To England nearer.

At last, when care had banished sleep,
    He saw one morning, dreaming, doting,
An empty hogshead from the deep
    Come shoreward floating.

He hid it in a cave, and wrought
    The live-long day laborious; lurking
Until he launched a tiny boat
    By mighty working.

Heaven help us ! 't was a thing beyond
    Description wretched; such a wherry
Perhaps ne'er ventured on a pond,
    Or crossed a ferry.

For ploughing in the salt-sea field,
    It would have made the boldest shudder;
Untarred, uncompassed, and unkeeled,—
    No sail, no rudder.

From neighboring woods he interlaced
    His sorry skiff with wattled willows;
And thus equipped he would have passed
    The foaming billows,—

But Frenchmen caught him on the beach,
    His little Argus sorely jeering;
The tidings of him chanced to reach
    Napoleon's hearing.

With folded arms Napoleon stood,
    Serene alike in peace and danger;
And, in his wonted attitude,
    Addressed the stranger:—

"Rash man, that wouldst yon Channel pass
    On twigs and staves so rudely fashioned,
Thy heart with some sweet British lass
    Must be impassioned."

"I have no sweetheart," said the lad;
    "But—absent long from one another—
Great was the longing that I had
    To see my mother."

"And so thou shalt," Napoleon said,
    "Ye've both my favor fairly won;
A noble mother must have bred
    So brave a son."

He gave the tar a piece of gold,
    And, with a flag of truce, commanded
He should be shipped to England Old,
    And safely landed.

Our sailor oft could scantly shift
    To find a dinner, plain and hearty,
But *never* changed the coin and gift
    Of Bonaparte.

➤✳THOUGHT.✳➤

BY CHRISTOPHER PEARSE CRANCH.

THOUGHT is deeper than all speech,
    Feeling deeper than all thought;
Souls to souls can never teach
    What unto themselves was taught.

We are spirits clad in veils;
    Man by man was never seen;
All our deep communing fails
    To remove the shadowy screen.

Heart to heart was never known;
    Mind with mind did never meet;
We are columns left alone
    Of a temple once complete.

Like the stars that gem the sky,
    Far apart though seeming near,
In our light we scattered lie;
    All is thus but starlight here.

What is social company
    But a babbling summer stream?
What our wise philosophy
    But the glancing of a dream?

Only when the sun of love
　　Melts the scattered stars of thought,
Only when we live above
　　What the dim-eyed world has taught.

Only when our souls are fed
　　By the fount which gave them birth,
And by inspiration led,
　　Which they never drew from earth,

We, like parted drops of rain,
　　Swelling till they meet and run,
Shall be all absorbed again,
　　Melting, flowing into one.

➜✳THE✦SEA✦FIGHT.✳←

AS TOLD BY AN ANCIENT MARINER.

ANONYMOUS.

AH, yes,—the fight ! Well, messmates, well,
    I served on board that Ninety-eight;
Yet what I saw I loathe to tell.
    To-night be sure a crushing weight
Upon my sleeping breast, a hell
    Of dread, will sit. At any rate,
Though land-locked here, a watch I'll keep,—
Grog cheers us still. Who cares for sleep?

That Ninety-eight I sailed on board;
    Along the Frenchman's coast we flew;
Right aft the rising tempest roared;
    A noble first rate hove in view;
And soon high in the gale there soared
    Her streamed-out bunting,—red, white, blue !
We cleared for fight, and landward bore,
To get between the chase and shore.

Masters, I cannot spin a yarn
  Twice laid with words of silken stuff.
A fact 's a fact; and ye may larn
  The rights o' this, though wild and rough
My words may loom. 'T is your consarn,
  Not mine, to understand. Enough;—
We neared the Frenchman where he lay,
And as we neared, he blazed away.

We tacked, hove to; we filled, we wore;
  Did all that seamanship could do
To rake him aft, or by the fore,—
  Now rounded off, and now broached to;
And now our starboard broadside bore,
  And showers of iron through and through
His vast hull hissed; our larboard then
Swept from his threefold decks his men.

As we, like a huge serpent, toiled,
  And wound about, through that wild sea,
The Frenchman each manœuvre foiled,—
  'Vantage to neither there could be.
Whilst thus the waves between us boiled,
  We both resolved right manfully
To fight it side by side;—began
Then the fierce strife of man to man.

Gun bellows forth to gun, and pain
  Rings out her wild, delirious scream !
Redoubling thunders shake the main;
  Loud crashing, falls the shot-rent beam.

The timbers with the broadsides strain;
   The slippery deck sends up a steam
From hot and living blood, and high
And shrill is heard the death-pang cry.

The shredded limb, the splintered bone,
   The unstiffened corpse, now block the way!
Who can hear the dying groan?
   The trumpet of the judgment-day,
Had it pealed forth its mighty tone,
   We should not then have heard,—to say
Would be rank sin; but this I tell,
That could alone our madness quell.

Upon the forcastle I fought
   As captain of the for'ad gun.
A scattering shot the carriage caught!
   What mother then had known her son
Of those who stood around?— distraught,
   And smeared with gore, about they run,
Then fall, and writhe, and howling die!
But one escaped,—that one was I!

Night darkened round, and the storm pealed;
   To windward of us lay the foe.
As he to leeward over keeled,
   He could not fight his guns below;
So just was going to strike,—when reeled
   Our vessel, as if some vast blow
From an Almighty hand had rent
The huge ship from her element.

Then howled the thunder. Tumult then
    Had stunned herself to silence. Round
Were scattered lightning-blasted men !
    Our mainmast went. All stifled, drowned,
Arose the Frenchman's shout. Again
    The bolt burst on us, and we found
Our masts all gone,--our decks all riven:
Man's war mocks faintly that of heaven !

Just then,—nay, messmates, laugh not now,—
    As I, amazed, one minute stood
Amidst that rout,—I know not how,—
    'T was silence all,—the raving flood,
The guns that pealed from stem to bow,
    And God's own thunder,—nothing could
I then of all that tumult hear,
Or see aught of all that scene of fear,—

My aged mother at her door
    Sat mildly o'er her humming wheel;
The cottage, orchard, and the moor,—
    I saw them plainly all. I 'll kneel,
And swear I saw them ! O, they wore
    A look all peace? Could I but feel
Again that bliss that then I felt,
That made my heart, like childhood's melt !

The blessed tear was on my cheek,
    She smiled with that old smile I know.
" Turn to me, mother, turn and speak,"
    Was on my quivering lips,—when lo !

All vanished, and a dark, red streak
    Glared wild and vivid from the foe,
That flashed upon the blood-stained water,—
For fore and aft the flames had caught her.

She struck and hailed us.   On us fast
    All burning, helplessly, she came,—
Near, and more near; and not a mast
    Had we to help us from that flame.
'T was then the bravest stood aghast,—
    'T was then the wicked, on the name
(With danger and with guilt appalled)
Of God, too long neglected, called.

The eddying flames with ravening tongue
    Now on our ship's dark bulwarks dash,—
We almost touched,—when ocean rung
    Down to its depths with one loud crash !
In heaven's top vault one instant hung
    The vast, intense, and blinding flash !
Then all was darkness, stillness, dread,—
The wave moaned over the valiant dead.

She's gone ! blown up ! that gallant foe !
    And though she left us in a plight,
We floated still; long were, I know,
    And hard, the labors of that night
To clear the wreck.   At length in tow
    A frigate took us, when 't was light;
And soon an English port we gained,—
A hulk all battered and blood-stained.

So many slain,—so many drowned!
 I like not of that fight to tell.
Come, let the cheerful grog go round!
 Messmates, I've done. A spell, ho! spell,—
Though a pressed man, I 'll still be found
 To do a seaman's duty well.
I wish our brother landsmen knew
One half we jolly tars go through.

➺✳ONLY·A·WOMAN.✳➻

BY DINAH MARIA MULOCK.

"She loves with love that cannot tire;
  And if, ah, woe! she loves alone,
Through passionate duty love flames higher,
  As grass grows taller round a stone."

COVENTRY PATMORE.

S O, the truth 's out.   I'll grasp it like a snake,—
It will not slay me.   My heart shall not break
Awhile, if only for the children's sake.

For his, too, somewhat.   Let him stand
    unblamed;
None say, he gave me less than honor claimed,
Except — one   trifle   scarcely   worth   being
    named —

The *heart*. That 's gone. The corrupt dead might be
As easily raised up, breathing,—fair to see,
As he could bring his whole heart back to me.

I never sought him in coquettish sport,
Or courted him as silly maidens court,
And wonder when the longed-for prize falls short.

I only loved him,—any woman would:
But shut my love up till he came and sued,
Then poured it o'er his dry life like a flood.

I was so happy I could make him blest !—
So happy that I was his first and best,
As he mine,—when he took me to his breast.

Ah me ! if only then he had been true !
If for one little year, a month or two,
He had given me love for love, as was my due !

Or had he told.me, ere the deed was done,
He only raised me to his heart's dear throne—
Poor substitute—because the queen was gone !

O, had he whispered, when his sweetest kiss
Was warm upon my mouth in fancied bliss,
He had kissed another woman even as this,—

It were less bitter ! Sometimes I could weep
To be thus cheated, like a child asleep;—
Were not my anguish far too dry and deep.

So I built my house upon another's ground;
Mocked with a heart just caught at the rebound,—
A cankered thing that looked so firm and sound.

And when that heart grew colder,—colder still,
I, ignorant, tried all duties to fulfil,
Blaming my foolish pain, exacting will,

All,—anything but him.   It was to.be
The full draught others drink up carelessly
Was made this bitter Tantalus-cup for me.

I say again,—he gives me all I claimed,
I and my children never shall be shamed:
He is a just man,—he will live unblamed.

Only—O God, O God, to cry for bread,
And get a stone !   Daily to lay my head
Upon a bosom where the old love's dead !

Dead ?—Fool !   It never lived.   It only stirred
Galvanic, like an hour-cold corpse.   None heard:
So let me bury it without a word.

He'll keep that other woman from my sight.
I know not if her face be foul or bright;
I only know that it was his delight—

As his was mine; I only know he stands
Pale, at the touch of their long-severed hands,
Then to a flickering smile his lips commands,

Lest I should grieve, or jealous anger show.
He need not.   When the ship's gone down, I trow,
We little reck whatever wind may blow.

And so my silent moan begins and ends,
No world's laugh or world's taunt, no pity of friends
Or sneer of foes, with this my torment blends.

None knows,—none heeds. I have a little pride;
Enough to stand up, wifelike, by his side,
With the same smile as when I was his bride;

And I shall take his children to my arms;
They will not miss these fading, worthless charms;
Their kiss—ah! unlike his—all pain disarms.

And haply as the solemn years go by,
He will think sometimes, with regretful sigh,
The other woman was less true than I.

✳ THE ✛ BELLS ✛ OF ✳ SHANDON ✳

BY FATHER PROUT.

Sabbata pango;
Funera plango;
Solemnia clango.

INSCRIPTION ON AN OLD BELL.

ITH deep affection
And recollection
I often think of
    Those Shandon bells,
Whose sounds so wild would,
In the days of childhood,
Fling round my cradle
    Their magic spells.

On this I ponder
Where'er I wander,
And thus grow fonder,
    Sweet Cork of thee,—
With thy bells of Shandon,
That sound so grand on
The pleasant waters
    Of the river Lee.

I 've heard bells chiming
Full many a clime in,
Tolling sublime in
    Cathedral shrine,
While at a glibe rate
Brass tongues would vibrate;
But all their music
    Spoke naught like thine.

For memory, dwelling
On each proud swelling
Of thy belfry, knelling
    Its bold notes free,
Made the bells of Shandon
Sound far more grand on
The pleasant waters
    Of the river Lee.

I 've heard bells tolling
Old Adrian's Mole in,
Their thunder rolling
    From the Vatican,—
And symbols glorious
Swinging uproarious
In the gorgeous turrets
    Of Notre Dame;

But thy sounds were sweeter
Than the dome of Peter
Flings o'er the Tiber,
    Pealing solemnly.

Oh! the bells of Shandon
Sound far more grand on
The pleasant waters
   Of the river Lee.

There 's a bell in Moscow;
While on tower and kiosk O
In St. Sophia
   The Turkman gets,
And loud in air
Calls men to prayer,
From the tapering summit
   Of tall minarets.

Such empty phantom
I freely grant them;
But there 's an anthem
   More dear to me,—
'T is the bells of Shandon,
That sound so grand on
The pleasant waters
   Of the river Lee.

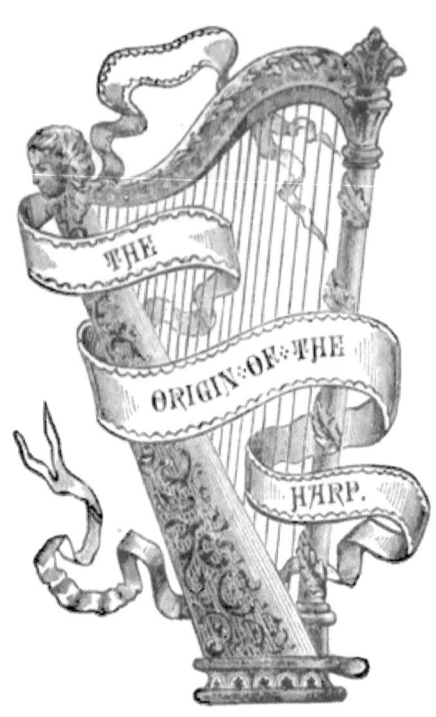

THE ORIGIN OF THE HARP.

BY THOMAS MOORE.

T is believed that this harp which I wake now for
    thee
Was a siren of old who sung under the sea;
And who often at eve through the bright billow
    roved
To meet on the green shore a youth whom she
    loved.

But she loved him in vain, for he left her to weep,
And in tears all the night her gold ringlets to steep,

Till Heaven looked with pity on true love so warm,
And changed to this soft harp the sea-maiden's form!

Still her bosom rose fair—still her cheek smiled the same—
While her sea-beauties gracefully curled round the frame;
And her hair, shedding tear-drops from all its bright rings,
Fell over her white arm, to make the gold strings!

Hence it came that this soft harp so long hath been known
To mingle love's language with sorrow's sad tone;
Till *thou* didst divide them, and teach the fond lay
To be love when I'm near thee and grief when away!

➤✴TO·MARY·IN·HEAVEN.✴◄

BY ROBERT BURNS.

[Composed by Burns, in September, 1789, on the anniversary of the day on which he heard of the death of his early love, Mary Campbell.]

THOU lingering star, with lessening ray,
    That lov'st to greet the early morn,
Again thou usher'st in the day
    My Mary from my soul was torn.
O Mary! dear departed shade!
    Where is thy place of blissful rest?
See'st thou thy lover lowly laid?
    Hear'st thou the groans that rend his breast?

That sacred hour can I forget,—
    Can I forget the hallowed grove,
Where by the winding Ayr we met
    To live one day of parting love!
Eternity will not efface
    Those records dear of transports past;
Thy image at our last embrace;
    Ah! little thought we 't was our last!

Ayr, gurgling, kissed his pebbled shore,
    O'erhung with wild woods, thickening green;
The fragrant birch, and hawthorn hoar,
    Twined amorous round the raptured scene;

The flowers sprang wanton to be prest,
    The birds sang love on every spray,—
Till soon, too soon, the glowing west
    Proclaimed the speed of winged day.

Still o'er these scenes my memory wakes,
    And fondly broods with miser care !
Time but the impression stronger makes,
    As streams their channels deeper wear
My Mary ! dear departed shade !
    Where is thy place of blissful rest ?
Seest thou thy lover lowly laid ?
    Hear'st thou the groans that rend his breast ?

THE SONGSTERS.

BY JAMES THOMSON.

PRISING the lark
Shrill-voiced and loud, the messenger of
morn:
Ere yet the shadows fly, he mounted sings
Amid the dawning clouds, and from their
haunts
Calls up the tuneful nations.   Every copse
Deep-tangled, tree irregular, and bush
Bending with dewy moisture, o'er the heads
Of the coy quiristers that lodge within,
Are prodigal of harmony.   The thrush
And woodlark, o'er the kind-contending throng

Superior heard, run through the sweetest length
Of notes; when listening Philomela deigns
To let them joy, and purposes, in thought
Elate, to make her night excel their day.
The blackbird whistles from the thorny brake;
The mellow bullfinch answers from the grove;
Nor are the linnets, o'er the flowering furze
Poured out profusely, silent: joined to these
Innumerous songsters, in the freshening shade
Of new-sprung leaves, their modulations mix
Mellifluous.   The jay, the rook, the daw,
And each harsh pipe, discordant heard alone,
Aid the full concert; while the stockdove breathes
A melancholy murmur through the whole.
    'T is love creates their melody, and all
This waste of music is the voice of love;
That even to birds and beasts the tender arts
Of pleasing teaches.

THE TWO APRIL MORNINGS.

BY WILLIAM WORDSWORTH.

E walked along, while bright and red
    Uprose the morning sun;
And Matthew stopped, he looked and said,
    "The will of God be done!"

A village schoolmaster was he,
    With hair of glittering gray;
As blithe a man as you could see
    On a spring holiday.

And on that morning, through the grass
    And by the steaming rills
We traveled merrily, to pass
    A day among the hills.

"Our work," said I, "was well begun;
    Then from thy breast what thought,
Beneath so beautiful a sun,
    So sad a sigh has brought?"

A second time did Matthew stop;
　　And, fixing still his eye
Upon the eastern mountain-top,
　　To me he made reply:

" Yon cloud with that long purple cleft
　　Brings fresh into my mind
A day like this, which I have left
　　Full thirty years behind.

" And just above yon slope of corn
　　Such colors, and no other,
Were in the sky that April morn,
　　Of this the very brother.

" With rod and line I sued the sport
　　Which that sweet season gave,
And, coming to the church, stopped short
　　Beside my daughter's grave.

" Nine summers had she scarcely seen,
　　The pride of all the vale;
And then she sang;—she would have been
　　A very nightingale.

" Six feet in earth my Emma lay;
　　And yet I loved her more—
For so it seemed—than till that day
　　I e'er had loved before.

" And, turning from her grave, I met
　　Beside the churchyard yew
A blooming girl, whose hair was wet
　　With points of morning dew.

"A basket on her head she bare;
　　Her brow was smooth and white:
To see a child so very fair,
　　It was a pure delight!

"No fountain from its rocky cave
　　E'er tripped with foot so free;
She seemed as happy as a wave
　　That dances on the sea.

"There came from me a sigh of pain
　　Which I could ill confine;
I looked at her, and looked again:
　　And did not wish her mine!"

—Matthew is in his grave, yet now
　　Methinks I see him stand
As at that moment, with a bough
　　Of wilding in his hand.

⇥✳ALPINE✦HEIGHTS.✳⇤

BY KRUMMACHER (GERMAN).

TRANSLATION OF CHARLES T. BROOKS.

ON Alpine heights the love of God is shed;
    He paints the morning red,
    The flowerets white and blue,
    And feeds them with his dew.
On Alpine heights a loving Father dwells.

On Alpine heights, o'er many a fragrant heath,
    The loveliest breezes breathe;
    So free and pure the air,
    His breath seems floating there.
On Alpine heights a loving Father dwells.

On Alpine heights, beneath his mild blue eye,
    Still vales and meadows lie;
    The soaring glacier's ice
    Gleams like a paradise.
On Alpine heights a loving Father dwells.

ALPINE HEIGHTS.

Down Alpine heights the silvery streamlets flow;
There the bold chamois go;
On giddy crags they stand,
And drink from his own hand.
On Alpine heights a loving Father dwells.

On Alpine heights the herdsman tends his herd;
His Shepherd is the Lord;
For he who feeds the sheep
Will sure his offspring keep.
On Alpine heights a loving Father dwells.

THE LANDING OF THE PILGRIM FATHERS.

BY FELICIA HEMANS.

THE breaking waves dashed high
    On a stern and rock-bound coast,
And the woods against a stormy sky
    Their giant branches tossed;

And the heavy night hung dark
    The hills and waters o'er,
When a band of exiles moored their bark
    On the wild New England shore.

Not as the conqueror comes,
    They, the true-hearted, came;
Not with the roll of the stirring drums,
    And the trumpet that sings of fame:

Not as the flying come,
    In silence and in fear;—
They shook the depths of the desert gloom
    With their hymns of lofty cheer.

Amidst the storm they sang,
    And the stars heard, and the sea;
And the sounding aisles of the dim woods rang
    To the anthem of the free.

The ocean eagle soared
    From his nest by the white waves foam,
And the rocking pines of the forest roared,—
    This was their welcome home.

There were men with hoary hair
    Amidst that pilgrim-band:
Why had they come to wither there,
    Away from their childhood's land?

There was woman's fearless eye,
    Lit by her deep love's truth;
There was manhood's brow serenely high,
    And the fiery heart of youth.

What sought they thus afar?
    Bright jewels of the mine?
The wealth of seas, the spoils of war?—
    They sought a faith's pure shrine!

Ay, call it holy ground,
    The soil where first they trod;
They have left unstained what there they found,—
    Freedom to worship God.

⋅➤✳SEVEN✳TIMES✳TWO.✳⬅

ROMANCE.

BY JEAN INGELOW.

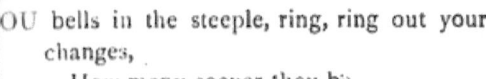

YOU bells in the steeple, ring, ring out your
    changes,
      How many soever they be,
And let the brown meadow-lark's note as
    he ranges
      Come over, come over to me.

Yet birds' clearest carol by fall or by
    swelling
      No magical sense conveys,
And bells have forgotten their old art of
    telling
      The fortune of future days.

"Turn again, turn again," once they rang cheerily
    While a boy listened alone:
Made his heart yearn again, musing so wearily
    All by himself on a stone.

Poor bells! I forgive you; your good days are over,
    And mine, they are yet to be;
No listening, no longing, shall aught, aught discover:
    You leave the story to me.

TO A SKELETON.

ANONYMOUS.

[The MSS. of this poem, which appeared during the first quarter of the present century, was said to have been found in the Museum of the Royal College of Surgeons, in London, near a perfect human skeleton, and to have been sent by the curator to the Morning Chronicle for publication. It excited so much attention that every effort was made to discover the author, and a responsible party went so far as to offer a reward of fifty guineas for information that would discover its origin. The author preserved his incognito, and, we believe, has never been discovered.]

BEHOLD this ruin! 'T was a skull
Once of ethereal spirit full.
This narrow cell was Life's retreat,
This space was Thought's mysterious seat.
What beauteous visions filled this spot,
What dreams of pleasure long forgot?
Nor hope, nor joy, nor love, nor fear,
Have left one trace of record here.

Beneath this mouldering canopy
Once shone the bright and busy eye,
But start not at the dismal void,—
If social love that eye employed,
If with no lawless fire it gleamed,
But through the dews of kindness beamed,
That eye shall be forever bright
When stars and sun are sunk in night.

Within this hollow cavern hung
The ready, swift, and tuneful tongue;
If Falsehood's honey is disdained,
And when it could not praise was chained;
If bold in Virtue's cause it spoke,
Yet gentle concord never broke,—
This silent tongue shall plead for thee
When Time unveils Eternity !

Say, did these fingers delve the mine ?
Or with the envied rubies shine ? .
To hew the rock or wear a gem
Can little now avail to them.
But if the page of Truth they sought,
Or comfort to a mourner brought,
These hands a richer meed shall claim
Than all that wait on Wealth and Fame.

Avails it whether bare or shod
These feet the paths of duty trod ?
If from the bowers of Ease they fled,
To seek Affliction's humble shed;
If Grandeur's guilty bride they spurned,
And home to Virtue's cot returned,—
These feet with angel wings shall vie,
And tread the palace of the sky !

➤✱IT✛NEVER✛COMES✛AGAIN.✱◄

BY RICHARD HENRY STODDARD.

THERE are gains for all our losses,
 There are balms for all our pains,
But when youth, the dream, departs,
It takes something from our hearts,
 And it never comes again.

We are stronger, and are better
 Under manhood's sterner reign;
Still we feel that something sweet
Followed youth, with flying feet,
 And will never come again.

Something beautiful is vanished,
 And we sigh for it in vain;
We behold it everywhere,
On the earth, and in the air,
 But it never comes again.

THE MODERN BELLE.

BY STARK.

SHE sits in a fashionable parlor,
    And rocks in her easy chair;
She is clad in silks and satins,
    And jewels are in her hair;
She winks and giggles and simpers,
    And simpers and giggles and winks;
And though she talks but little,
    'T is a good deal more than she thinks.

She lies abed in the morning
    Till nearly the hour of noon,
Then comes down snapping and snarling
    Because she was called so soon;
Her hair is still in papers,
    Her cheeks still fresh with paint,—
Remains of her last night's blushes,
    Before she intended to faint.

She dotes upon men unshaven,
    And men with "flowing hair";
She 's eloquent over mustaches,
    They give such a foreign air.

She talks of Italian music,
    And falls in love with the moon;
And, if a mouse were to meet her,
    She would sink away in a swoon.

Her feet are so very little,
    Her hands are so very white,
Her jewels so very heavy,
    And her head so very light;
Her color is made of cosmetics
    (Though this she will never own),
Her body is made mostly of cotton,
    Her heart is made wholly of stone.

She falls in love with a fellow
    Who swells with a foreign air;
He marries her for her money,
    She marries him for his hair!
One of the very best matches,—
    Both are well mated in life;
She 's got a fool for a husband,
    He 's got a fool for a wife!

➤✳KISSING 'S✛NO✛SIN.✳◄

ANONYMOUS.

OME say that kissing 's a sin;
  But I think it 's nane ava,
For kissing has wonn'd in this world
  Since ever that there was twa.

O, if it wasna lawfu',
  Lawyers wadna allow it;
If it wasna holy,
  Ministers wadna do it.

If it wasna modest,
  Maidens wadna tak' it;
If it wasna plenty,
  Puir folk wadna get it.

LESSONS FOR LIFE.

THOU whom chance may hither lead,
Be thou clad in rustic weed,
Be thou deck'd in silken stole,
'Grave these counsels on thy soul.
  Life is but a day at most,
Sprung from night, in darkness lost;
Hope not sunshine every hour,
Fear not clouds will always lower.
  As Youth and Love, with sprightly **dance,**
Beneath thy morning-star advance,
Pleasure, with her siren air,
May delude the thoughtless pair:
Let Prudence bless Enjoyment's cup,
Then raptured sip, and sip it up.
  As thy day grows warm and high,
Life's meridian flaming nigh,
Dost thou spurn the humble vale?
Life's proud summits wouldst thou scale?
Check thy climbing step, elate,
Evils lurk in felon wait:
Dangers, eagle-pinion'd, bold,
Soar around each cliffy hold,
While cheerful Peace, with linnet song,
Chants the lowly dells among.
  As the shades of evening close,
Beckoning thee to long repose;

As Life itself becomes disease,
Seek the chimney-nook of ease.
There ruminate with sober thought,
On all thou'st seen, and heard, and wrought;
And teach the sportive younkers round,
. Saws of experience, sage and sound.
Say, man's true, genuine estimate,
The grand criterion of his fate,
Is not—Art thou high or low?
Did thy fortune ebb or flow?
Wast thou cottager or king?
Peer or peasant?— No such thing!
Did many talents gild thy span?
Or frugal nature grudge thee one?
Tell them, and press it on their mind,
As thou thyself must shortly find,
The smile or frown of awful Heaven,
To Virtue or to Vice is given.
Say, "To be just, and kind, and wise,
There solid self-enjoyment lies;
That foolish, selfish, faithless ways,
Lead to the wretched, vile and base."

    Thus resign'd and quiet, creep
To the bed of lasting sleep;
Sleep, whence thou shalt ne'er awake,
Night, where dawn shall never break,
Till future life, future no more,
To light and joy the good restore,
To light and joy unknown before.
    Stranger go! Heaven be thy guide!
Quoth the beadsman of Nithside.*

---

*These beautiful lines were written in " Friars-Carse " Hermitage, on
the banks of the Nith.

❧LETTERS.❧

BY RALPH WALDO EMERSON.

VERY day brings a ship,
Every ship brings a word;
Well for those who have no fear,
Looking seaward well assured
That the word the vessel brings
Is the word they wish to hear.

➤✳HYMN.✳⬅

BY HAWKESWORTH.

N Sleep's serene oblivion laid,
    I safely passed the silent night;
At once I see the breaking shade,
    And drink again the morning light.

New-born I bless the waking hour,
    Once more, with awe, rejoice *to be;*
My conscious soul resumes her power,
    And springs, my gracious God, to Thee.

O, guide me through the various maze
    My doubtful feet are doom'd to tread;
And spend Thy shield's protecting blaze,
    When dangers press around my head.

A *deeper shade* will soon impend, ·
    A *deeper sleep* my eyes oppress;
Yet still Thy strength shall me defend,
    Thy goodness still shall deign to bless.

That *deeper shade* shall fade away,
    That *deeper sleep* shall leave my eyes;
Thy *light* shall give eternal day!
    Thy *love* the rapture of the skies!

GOLD.

BY ABRAHAM COWLEY.

A MIGHTY pain to love it is,
And 't is a pain that love to miss,
But, of all pains, the greatest pain
It is to love, but Love in vain.
Virtue now nor noble blood,
Nor wit, by love is understood.
Gold alone does passion move!
Gold monopolizes love!
A curse on her and on the man
Who this traffic first began!
A curse on him who found the ore!
A curse on him who digg'd the store!
A curse on him who did refine it!
A curse on him who first did coin it!
A curse, all curses else above,
On him who used it first in love!
Gold begets in brethren hate;
Gold, in families, debate;
Gold does friendship separate;
Gold does civil wars create.
These the smallest harms of it;
Gold, alas! does love beget.

➤✳THE✦VILLAGE✦PREACHER.✳⬅

FROM THE DESERTED VILLAGE.

BY OLIVER GOLDSMITH.

NEAR yonder copse, where once the garden
   smiled,
And still where many a garden flower grows
   wild;
There, where a few torn shrubs the place
   disclose,
The village preacher's modest mansion rose.
A man he was to all the country dear,
And passing rich with forty pounds a year;
Remote from towns he ran his godly race,
Nor ne'er had changed, nor wish'd to change his place;
Unskilful he to fawn, or seek for power
By doctrines fashion'd to the varying hour;
Far other aims his heart had learn'd to prize,
More bent to raise the wretched than to rise.
His house was known to all the vagrant train,
He chid their wanderings, but relieved their pain;
The long-remember'd beggar was his guest,
Whose beard descending swept his aged breast;
The ruin'd spendthrift, now no longer proud,

Claim'd kindred there, and had his claims allow'd;
The broken soldier, kindly bade to stay,
Sat by his fire, and talk'd the night away;
Wept o'er his wounds, or, tales of sorrow done,
Shoulder'd his crutch, and show'd how fields were won.
Pleased with his guests, the good man learn'd to grow,
And quite forgot their vices in their woe;
Careless their merits or their faults to scan,
His pity gave ere charity began.

 Thus to relieve the wretched was his pride,
And e'en his failings lean'd to Virtue's side;
But in his duty prompt at every call,
He watch'd and wept, he pray'd and felt for all.
And, as a bird each fond endearment tries,
To tempt its new-fledged offspring to the skies;
He tried each art, reproved each dull delay,
Allured to brighter worlds, and led the way.

 Beside the bed where parting life was laid,
And sorrow, guilt, and pain, by turns dismay'd,
The reverend champion stood. At his control,
Despair and anguish fled the struggling soul;
Comfort came down the trembling wretch to raise,
And his last faltering accents whispered praise.

 At church, with meek and unaffected grace,
His looks adorn'd the venerable place;
Truth from his lips prevail'd with double sway.
And fools, who came to scoff, remain'd to pray.
The service past, around the pious man,
With ready zeal, each honest rustic ran;
E'en children follow'd with endearing wile,
And pluck'd his gown, to share the good man's smile.
His ready smile a parent's warmth exprest,
Their welfare pleased him, and their cares distrest;

To them his heart, his love, his griefs were given,
But all his serious thoughts had rest in heaven:
As some tall cliff that lifts its awful form,
Swells from the vale, and midway leaves the storm,
Though round its breast the rolling clouds are spread,
Eternal sunshine settles on its head.

→⁕LITTLE⁕BREECHES.⁕←

A PIKE COUNTY VIEW OF SPECIAL PROVIDENCE.

BY JOHN HAY.

DON'T go much on religion,
 I never ain't had no show;
But I've got a middlin' tight grip, sir,
 On the handful o' things I know.
I don't pan out on the prophets
 And free-will, and that sort of thing,—
But I b'lieve in God and the angels,
 Ever sence one night last spring.

I come into town with some turnips,
 And my little Gabe came along,—
No four-year-old in the county
 Could beat him for pretty and strong.
Peart and chipper and sassy,
 Always ready to swear and fight,—
And I 'd larnt him ter chaw terbacker,
 Just to keep his milk-teeth white.

The snow come down like a blanket
 As I passed by Taggart's store;
I went in for a jug of molasses
 And left the team at the door.

They scared at something and started,—
    I heard one little squall,
And hell-to-split over the prairie
    Went team, Little Breeches and all.

Hell-to-split over the prairie !
    I was almost froze with skeer;
But we rousted up some torches,
    And searched for 'em far and near.
At last we struck hosses and wagon,
    Snowed under a soft white mound,
Upsot, dead beat,—but of little Gabe
    No hide nor hair was found.

And here all hope soured on me
    Of my fellow-critter's aid,—
I jest flopped down on my marrow-bones,
    Crotch-deep in the snow, and prayed.

By this, the torches was played out,
    And me and Isrul Parr
Went off for some wood to a sheepfold
    That he said was somewhar thar.

We found it at last, and a little shed
    Where they shut up the lambs at night.
We looked in, and seen them huddled thar,
    So warm and sleepy and white;
And THAR sot Little Breeches and chirped,
    As peart as ever you see,
"I want a chaw of terbacker,
    And that's what's the matter of me."

How did he git thar? Angels.
　　He could never have walked in that storm.
They jest scooped down and toted him
　　To whar it was safe and warm.
And I think that saving a little child,
　　And bringing him to his own,
Is a darned sight better business
　　Than loafing around The Throne.

→✳THE✦FISHERMEN.✳←

BY CHARLES KINGSLEY.

THREE fishers went sailing out into the west—
    Out into the west as the sun went down;
    Each thought of the woman who loved him the
        best,
    And the children stood watching them out of
        the town.
For men must work, and women must weep;
And there 's little to earn, and many to keep,
    Though the harbor bar be moaning.

Three wives sat up in the lighthouse tower,
    And trimmed the lamps as the sun went down;
And they looked at the squall, and they looked at the shower,
    And the rack it came rolling up, ragged and brown;
But men must work, and women must weep,
Though storms be sudden, and waters deep,
    And the harbor bar be moaning.

Three corpses lay out in the shining sands
    In the morning gleam as the tide went down;
And the women are watching and wringing their hands,
    For those who will never come back to the town;
For men must work, and women must weep,—
And the sooner it 's over, the sooner to sleep,—
    And good by to the bar and its moaning.

THE FISHER BOY.

⋆∷ADDRESS∷TO∷THE∷OCEAN∷⋆

BY BARRY CORNWALL.

O THOU vast Ocean! ever-sounding Sea!
Thou symbol of a drear immensity!
Thou thing that windest round the solid world
Like a huge animal, which, downward hurled
From the black clouds, lies weltering and alone,
Lashing and writhing till its strength be gone!

Thy voice is like the thunder, and thy sleep
Is as a giant's slumber, loud and deep.
Thou speakest in the east and in the west
At once, and on thy heavily laden breast
Fleets come and go, and shapes that have no life
Or motion, yet are moved and meet in strife.
The earth has naught of this: no chance or change
Ruffles its surface, and no spirits dare
Give answer to the tempest-wakened air;
But o'er its wastes the weakly tenants range
At will, and wound its bosom as they go:
Ever the same, it hath no ebb, no flow:
But in their stated rounds the seasons come,
And pass like visions to their wonted home;
And come again, and vanish; the young Spring
Looks ever bright with leaves and blossoming;
And Winter always winds his sullen horn,
When the wild Autumn, with a look forlorn,
Dies in his stormy manhood; and the skies
Weep, and flowers sicken, when the summer flies.
O, wonderful thou art, great element,
And fearful in thy spleeny humors bent,
And lovely in repose! thy summer form
Is beautiful, and when thy silver waves
Make music in earth's dark and winding caves,
I love to wander on thy pebbled beach,
Marking the sunlight at the evening hour,
And hearken to the thoughts thy waters teach,—
Eternity — Eternity.— and Power.

DR. ADDISON ALEXANDER'S MONOSYLLABLE
❖ POEM. ❖

[The following curious illustration of the power of words in the English language has long been out of print]:—

THINK not that strength lies in the big, round word,
  Or that the brief and plain must needs be weak.
To whom can this be true who once has heard
  The cry for help, the tongue that all men speak
When want, or woe, or fear is in the throat,
  So that each word gasped out is like a shriek
Press'd from the sore heart, or a strange, wild note,
  Sung by some fay or fiend ! There is a strength
Which dies if stretched too far or spun too fine,
  Which has more height than breadth, more depth than
    length.
Let but this force of thought and speech be mine,
  And he that will may take the sleek, fat phrase,
Which glows and burns not, though it gleam and shine;
  Light, but not heat—a flash without a blaze.

Nor is it mere strength that the short word boasts:
  It serves of more than fight or storm to tell—
The roar of waves that clash on rock-bound coasts,
  The crash of tall trees when the wild winds swell,

The roar of guns, the groans of men that die
    On blood-stained fields. It has a voice as well
For them that far off on their sick beds lie,
    For them that weep, for them that mourn the dead,
For them that laugh, and dance, and clap their hand;
    To joy's quick step, as well as grief's low tread.
The sweet, plain words we learnt at first keep time,
    And though the theme be sad, or gay, or grand,
With each, with all, these may be made to chime,
    In thought, or speech, or song, or prose, or rhyme.

→✳SONG✛OF✛THE✛DECANTER..✳←

There was an old decanter,
and its mouth was gaping
wide; the rosy wine
had ebbed away
and left
its crys-
tal side;
and the wind
went humming,
humming;
up and
down the
sides it flew,
and through the
reed-like,
hollow neck
the wildest notes it
blew. I placed it in the
window, where the blast was
blowing free, and fancied that its
pale mouth sang the queerest strains
to me. "They tell me — puny conquerors! — the Plague has slain his ten,
and War his hundred thousands of the
very best of men; but I " — 'twas thus
the bottle spoke — "but I have con-
quered more than all your famous conquerors, so feared and famed of yore.
Then come, ye youths and maidens,
come drink from out my cup, the bev-
erage that dulls the brain and burns
the spirit up; that puts to shame
the conquerors that slay their
scores below, for this has del-
uged millions with the lava
tide of woe. Though in the
path of battle, darkest
waves of blood may roll,
yet while I killed the body
I have damned the very
soul. The cholera, the
sword, such ruin never
wrought, as I, in mirth or
malice, on the innocent have
brought. And still I breathe
upon them, and they shrink
before my breath; and year
by year my thousands tread
THE TERRIBLE ROAD TO DEATH.

LINES AND COUPLETS.

FROM POPE.

WHAT, and how great the virtue of the art,
To live on little with a cheerful heart.

Between excess and famine lies a mean,
Plain, but not sordid, though not splendid, clean.

Its proper power to hurt each creature feels:
Bulls aim their horns, and asses kick their heels.

Here Wisdom calls, "Seek virtue first, be bold;
As gold to silver, virtue is to gold."

Let lands and houses have what lords they will,
Let us be fixed and our own masters still.

'T is the first virtue vices to abhor,
And the first wisdom to be fool no more.

Long as to him who works for debt, the day.

Not to go back is somewhat to advance,
And men must walk, at least, before they dance.

———

True, conscious honor is to feel no sin;
He 's armed without that 's innocent within.

———

For virtue's self may too much zeal be had,
The worst of madmen is a saint run mad.

———

If wealth alone can make and keep us blest,
Still, still be getting; never, never rest.

———

That God of nature who within us still
Inclines our actions, not constrains our will.

———

It is not poetry, but prose run mad.

———

Pretty in amber to observe the forms
Of hair, or straws, or dirt, or grubs, or worms;
The things, we know, are neither rich nor rare,
But wonder how the mischief they got there !

———

Do good by stealth, and blush to find it fame.

———

Curst be the verse, how well soe'er it flow,
That tends to make one honest man my foe.

Who shames a scribbler? Break one cobweb through,
He spins the slight, self-pleasing thread anew;
Destroy his fib or sophistry, in vain,
The creature's at his dirty work again,
Throned in the centre of his thin designs,
Proud of a vast extent of flimsy lines.

He who, still wanting, though he lives on theft,
Steals much, spends little, yet has nothing left.

What future bliss He gives thee not to know,
But gives that hope to be thy blessing now.

All nature is but art, unknown to thee,
All chance, direction which thou canst not see.

'T is education forms the common mind;
Just as the twig is bent the tree 's inclined.

Manners with fortunes, humors turn with climes,
Tenets with books, and principles with times.

Who shall decide when doctors disagree?

And then mistook reverse of wrong for right.

That secret rare between the extremes to move,
Of mad good-nature and of mean self-love.

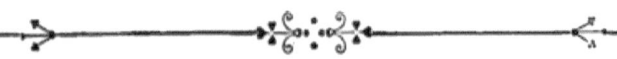

Ye little stars, hide your diminished rays.

———

Who builds a church to God, and not to fame,
Will never mark the marble with his name.

———

'T is strange the music should his cares employ
To gain those riches he can ne'er enjoy.

———

Something there is more needful than expense,
And something previous e'en to taste, — 't is sense.

———

In all let Nature never be forgot,
But treat the goddess like a modest fair,
Not over-dress nor leave her wholly bare;
Let not each beauty everywhere be spied,
Where half the skill is decently to hide.

➤ ⁂ ALBUM ✠ VERSES. ⁂ ◀

THERE are ten thousand tones and signs
We hear and see, but none defines—
Involuntary sparks of thought
Which strike from out the heart o'erwrought,
And form a strange intelligence
Alike mysterious and intense;
Which link the burning chain that binds,
Without their will, young hearts and minds,
Conveying, as an electric wire,
We know not how, the absorbing fire.

BYRON.

LOVE is not love
Which alters when its alteration finds,
Or bends with the remover to remove:
O no! it is an ever fixed mark,
That looks on tempests, and is never shaken;
It is the star to every wandering bark,
Whose worth 's unknown, although its height be taken.

SHAKESPEARE.

THERE is a comfort in the strength of Love;
'T will make a thing endurable, which else
Would overset the brain, or break the heart.

WORDSWORTH.

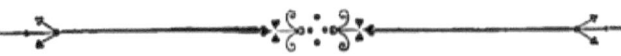

FAREWELL, oh farewell, but whenever you give
    A thought to the days that are gone,
Of the bright sunny things that in memory live
    Let a thought of the writer be one.
The hope is but humble—he asks but a share,
    But a part of *thy memories* to be,
While no *future* to *him* can in rapture compare
    To the past, made enchanting by thee.

SAMUEL LOVER.

THE joys of life are heightened by a friend;
The woes of life are lessened by a friend;
In all the cares of life, we by a friend
Assistance find — who'd be without a friend?

WANDESFORD.

WHY should I blush to own I love?
'T is Love that rules the realms above.
Why should I blush to say to all
That virtue holds my heart in thrall?

Why should I seek the thickest shade,
Lest Love's dear secret be betrayed?
Why the stern brow deceitful move,
When I am languishing with love?

Is it a weakness thus to dwell
On passions that I dare not tell?
Such weakness I would ever prove.
'T is painful, but 't is sweet to love!

HENRY KIRKE WHITE.

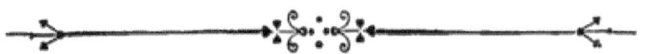

" I will not say I'd give the world
　　To win those charms divine;
I will not say I'd give the world—
　　The world it is not mine.
The vow that's made thy love to win
　　In simple truth shall be;
My heart is all I have to give,
　　And give that all to thee."

But while I knelt at beauty's shrine,
　　And love's devotion paid,
I felt 't was but an empty vow
　　That passion's pilgrim made;
For while, in raptur'd gazing lost,
　　To give my heart I swore,
One glance from her soon made me feel
　　My heart was mine no more.

SAMUEL LOVER.

Friendship is power and riches all to me;
Friendship 's another element of life;
Water and fire not of more general use
To the support and comfort of the world
Than Friendship to the being of my joy:
. I would do everything to secure a friend.

Silence in love betrays more woe
　　Than words, though ne'er so witty;
A beggar that is dumb, you know,
　　Deserves a double pity.

SIR HENRY WOTTON.

THE dart of Love was feather'd first
  From Folly's wing, they say,
Until he tried his shaft to shoot
  In Beauty's heart one day;
He miss'd the maid so oft, 't is said,
  His aim became untrue,
And Beauty laugh'd, as his last shaft
  He from his quiver drew;
"In vain," said she, "you shoot at me,
  You little spiteful thing—
The feather on your shaft I scorn,
  When pluck'd from Folly's wing."

But Cupid soon fresh arrows found
  And fitted to his string,
And each new shaft he feather'd from
  His own bright glossy wing;
He shot until no plume was left
  To waft him to the sky,
And Beauty smiled upon the child,
  When he no more could fly;
" Now, Cupid, I am thine," she said,
  " Leave off thy archer play,
For Beauty yields—when she is sure
  Love will not fly away."

SAMUEL LOVER.

Our grandsire, ere of Eve possess'd,
Alone, and e'en in Paradise unblest,
With mournful looks the blissful scene surveyed,
And wandered in the solitary shade;
The Maker saw, took pity, and bestowed
Woman, the last, the best reserved of God.

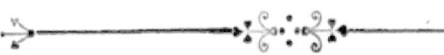

I HOLD it true, whate'er befall—
   I feel it when I sorrow most—
   'T is better to have loved and lost,
Than never to have loved at all.

TENNYSON.

To Woman, whose best books are human hearts,
Wise Heaven a genius less profound imparts;
His awful—hers is lovely; his should tell
How thunderbolts, and hers how roses fell.
Her rapid mind decides while his debates;
She feels a truth that he but calculates.
He, provident, averts approaching ill;
She snatches present good with ready skill.
That active perseverance his, which gains;
And hers, that passive patience which sustains.

BARRETT.

YES!   Love indeed is light from heaven,
   A spark of that immortal fire
With angels shared—to mortals given,
   To lift from earth our low desire.
Devotion wafts the mind above,
But heaven itself descends in love;
A feeling from the Godhead caught,
To wean from self each sordid thought;
A ray of Him who formed the whole;
A glory circling round the soul.

BYRON.

LOVE is a subject to himself alone,
And knows no other empire than his own.

· LANSDOWNE.

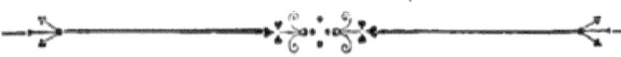

LIVES there the man too cold to prove
The joys of Friendship and of Love?
Then let him die; when these are fled,
Scarce do we differ from the dead.

AFIZ.

ALBUMS are records, kept by gentle dames,
To show us that their friends can write their names;
That Miss can draw, or brother John can write
"Sweet lines," or that they know a Mr. White.
The lady comes, with lowly grace upon her.
"'T will be so kind," and "do her book such honor;"
We bow, smile, deprecate, protest, read o'er
The names to see what has been done before,
Wish to say something wonderful, but can't,
And write, with modest glory, "William Grant."
Johnson succeeds, and Thompson, Jones, and Clarke,
And Cox with an original remark
Out of the speaker;—then come John's "sweet lines,"
Fanny's "sweet airs," and Jenny's "sweet designs:"
Then Hobbs, Cobbs, Dodds, Lord Strut, and Lady Brisk,
And, with a flourish underneath him, Fisk.

Alas! why sit I here, committing jokes
On social pleasures and good-humor'd folks,
That see far better with their trusting eyes,
Than all the blinkings of the would-be wise?
Albums are, after all, pleasant inventions,
Make friends more friendly, grace one's good intentions,
Brighten dull names, give great ones kindred looks,
Nay, now and then produce right curious books,
And make the scoffer (now the case with me)
Blush to look round on deathless company.

LEIGH HUNT.

BEWARE of sudden friendship; 't is a flower
That thrives but in the sun; its bud is fair,
And it may blossom in the summer hour,
But winter's withering tempests will not bear.
True Friendship is a tree, whose lasting strength
Is slow of growth, but proves, whate'er befall,
Through life our hope and haven, and at length
Yields but to death—the power that conquers all.

As o'er the cold sepulchral stone
    Some name arrests the passer-by,
Thus, when thou view'st this page alone,
    May mine attract thy pensive eye!
And when by thee that name is read,
    Perchance in some succeeding year,
Reflect on me as on the dead,
    And think my heart is buried here.

BYRON.

HERE is one leaf reserved for me,
From all thy sweet memories free;
And here my simple song might tell
The feelings thou must guess so well.
But could I thus within thy mind
One little vacant corner find,
Where no impression yet is seen,
Where no memorial yet has been;
O, it should be my sweetest care
To write my name forever there!

T. MOORE.

A PEPPER-CORN is very small, but seasons every dinner
More than all other condiments, although 't is sprinkled
    thinner;
Just so a little Woman is, if Love will let you win her—
There 's not a joy in all the world you will not find within
    her.

And as within the little rose you find the richest dyes,
And in the little grain of gold much price and value lies,
As from a little balsam much odor doth arise,
So in a little Woman there 's a taste of paradise.

                FROM THE SPANISH OF DE HITA.

YE are stars of the night, ye are gems of the morn,
Ye are dewdrops whose lustre illumines the thorn;
And rayless that night is, that morning unblest,
When no beams in your eye light up peace in the breast.
And the sharp thorn of sorrow sinks deep in the heart,
Till the sweet lip of Woman assuages the smart;
'T is hers o'er the couch of misfortune to bend,
In fondness a lover, in firmness a friend;
And prosperity's hour, be it ever confessed,
From Woman receives both refinement and zest;
And adorn'd by the bays or enwreath'd with the willow,
Her smile is our need, and her bosom our pillow.

LOVE! What a volume in a word! an ocean in a tear!
A seventh heaven in a glance! a whirlwind in a sigh!
The lightning in a touch—a millennium in a moment!
What concentrated joy, or woe, in blest or blighted love!

                TUPPER.

DIE when you will, you need not wear
At heaven's court a form more fair
    Than beauty here on earth has given.
Keep but the lovely looks we see—
The voice we hear—and you will be
    An angel *ready made* for heaven.

I HAVE seen the wild flowers springing,
    In wood, and field, and glen,
Where a thousand birds were singing,
    And my thoughts were of thee then;
For there 's nothing gladsome round me,
    Or beautiful to see,
Since thy beauty's spell has bound me,
    But is eloquent of thee.

                    RICHARD HOWITT.

FRIEND after friend departs;
    Who hath not lost a friend?
There is no union here of hearts
    That finds not here an end.
Were this frail world our only rest,
Living or dying, none were blest.

Thus star by star declines,
    Till all are passed away,
As morning high and higher shines
    To pure and perfect day;
Nor sink those stars in empty night,
They lose themselves in heaven's own light.

                    MONTGOMERY.

Doubt thou the stars are fire;
    Doubt that the sun doth move;
Doubt Truth to be a liar;
    But never doubt I love !

SHAKESPEARE.

For me I'm woman's slave confessed—
Without her, hopeless and unblest:
And so are all, gainsay who can,
For what would be the life of man,
If left in desert or in isle,
Unlightened up by beauty's smile ?
Even tho' he boasted monarch's name,
And o'er his own sex reign'd supreme,
With thousands bending to his sway,
If lovely Woman were away,
What were his life ?   What could it be ?
A vapor on a shoreless sea;
A troubled cloud in darkness toss'd,
Amongst the waste of waters lost;
A ship deserted in the gale,
Without a steersman or a sail,
A star, or beacon-light before,
Or hope of haven evermore;
A thing without a human tie,
Unloved to live,—unwept to die.

HOGG.

Oh, fairest of creation ! last and best
Of all God's works ! creature in whom excelled
Whatever can to sight or thought be form'd
Holy, divine, good, amiable, or sweet !

MILTON.

I HAVE heard of reasons manifold
   Why Love must needs be blind;
But this the best of all I hold—
   His eyes are in his mind.

What outward form and feature are
   He guesseth but in part;
But what within is good and fair
   He seeth with the heart.

S. T. COLERIDGE.

WOMAN'S truth and woman's love
   Trusting ever,
   Faithless never,
Blest on earth, is blest above.

Ministering oft in sorrow's hour,
   ' Loving truly,
   Fondly, duly
Proving e'er affection's power.

Ne'er forgetting, ne'er forgot;
   Richest treasures,
   Joyful pleasures
Ever be her happy lot.

THE light that beams from Woman's eye,
   And sparkles through her tear,
Responds to that impassion'd sigh
   Which love delights to hear.
'T is the sweet language of the soul,
   On which a voice is hung,
More eloquent than ever stole
   From saint's or poet's tongue.

THE sunshine of the heart be mine,
    That beams a charm around;
Where'er it sheds its ray divine,
    Is all enchanted ground !
No fiend of care may enter there,
    Tho' Fate employ her art:—
Her power, tho' mighty, bows to *thine*,
    Bright sunshine of the heart !

SAMUEL LOVER.

FAITH is the star that gleams above,
    Hope is the flower that buds below;
Twin tokens of celestial love
    That out from Nature's bosom grow;
And still alike, in sky, on sod,
That star and blossom ever point to God.

KENT.

As half in shade, and half in sun,
    This world along its path advances,
Oh ! may that side the sun shines on
    Be all that ever meets thy glances;
May Time, who casts his blight on all,
    And daily dooms some joy to death,
On thee let years so gently fall
    They shall not crush one flower beneath.

MOORE.

LONGEST joys won't last forever—
    Make the most of every day;
Youth and beauty Time will sever,
    But Content hath no decay.

Ye flowers that droop, forsaken by the spring;
Ye birds that, forsaken by the summer, cease to sing;
Ye trees that fade when autumn heats remove,
Say, is not Absence death to those who love?

POPE.

Not purple violets in the early spring
Such graceful sweets, such tender beauties bring;
The orient blush which does thy cheeks adorn,
Makes coral pale—vies with the rosy morn.

LEE.

This is the charm, by sages often told,
Converting all it touches into gold;
Content can soothe, where'er by fortune placed,
Can rear a garden in a desert waste.

HENRY KIRKE WHITE.

Duty has pleasures with no satiety.
Duties fulfilled are always pleasures to the memory.
Duty makes pleasure doubly sweet by contrast.

HALIBURTON.

There is a jewel which no Indian mine can buy,
No chemic art can counterfeit;
It makes men rich in greatest poverty,
Makes water wine, turns wooden cups to gold,
The homely whistle to sweet music's strain;
Seldom it comes—to few from Heaven sent—
That much in little—all in thought—Content.

WILBYE.

HOPE is the lover's staff:
Walk thou with that,
And manage it against despairing thought.
SHAKESPEARE.

———

O GRANT me, Heav'n, a middle state,
Neither too humble nor too great;
More than enough for nature's ends,
With something left to treat my friends.
MALLET.

———

WHAT will it matter
By and by,
Whether our path below was bright;
Whether it shone through dark or light—
Under a gray or golden sky—
What will it matter,
By and by?

———

THOU'RT fairer than the poets can express,
Or happy painters fancy when they love.
OTWAY.

———

LOVE is to my impassion'd soul
Not, as with others, a mere part
Of its existence; but the whole—
The very life-breath of my heart.

———

So like the chances are of Love and War,
That they alone in this distinguished are:
In Love, the victors from the vanquished fly—
They fly that wound, and they pursue that die.
WALLER.

In Christian world Mary the garland wears !
Rebecca sweetens on a Hebrew ear;
Quakers for pure Priscilla are more clear;
And the light Gaul by amorous Ninon swears.
Among the lesser lights how Lucy shines !
What air of fragrance Rosamond throws round !
How like a hymn doth sweet Cecilia sound !
Of Marthas and of Abigails few lines
Have bragg'd in verse.   Of coarsest household stuff
Should homely Joan be fashion'd.   But can
You Barbara resist, or Marian ?
And is not Clare for love excuse enough ?
Yet, by my faith in numbers, I profess
These all than Saxon Edith please me less.

CHARLES LAMB.

SMALL service is true service where it lasts:
    Of friends, however, scorn not one:
The daisy, by the shadow that it casts,
    Protects the lingering dew-drop from the sun.

WELL chosen friendship, the most noble
Of virtues, all our joys makes double,
And into halves divides our trouble.

LOVE reckons hours for months, and days for years;
And every little absence is an age.

DRYDEN.

A THING of beauty is a joy forever;
Its loveliness increases; it will never
Pass into nothingness.

KEATS.

THEY say that Love had once a book
    (The urchin likes to copy you)
Where all who came the pencil took,
    And wrote, like us, a line or two.

'T was innocence, the maid divine,
    Who kept this volume bright and fair,
And saw that no unhallowed line
    Or thought profane should enter there.

Beneath the touch of Hope, how soft,
    How light the magic pencil ran!
Till Fear would come, alas! as oft,
    And, trembling, close what Hope began.

A tear or two had dropped from Grief;
    And Jealousy would, now and then,
Ruffle in haste some snowy leaf,
    Which Love had still to smooth again.

But oh! there was a blooming boy
    Who often turned the pages o'er,
And wrote therein such words of joy
    As all who read still sighed for more.

And Pleasure was this spirit's name;
    And though so soft his voice and look,
Yet Innocence, whene'er he came,
    Would tremble for her spotless book!

For oh! 't would make you weep to see
    How Pleasure's honeyed hand had torn
And stained the page where Modesty
    A rose's bud had freshly drawn.

And Fancy's emblems lost their glow;
    And Hope's sweet lines were all defaced:
And Love himself could hardly know
    What Love himself had lately traced.

Beware of Pleasure and his lures;
    In virtue's ranks he finds no place.
Those pleasures only should be yours
      That spring from thoughts and deeds of grace.

                  ADAPTED FROM MOORE.

www.ingramcontent.com/pod-product-compliance
Lightning Source LLC
Chambersburg PA
CBHW021049030726
47496CB00006B/1762